"We all know who started that fire!"

Sheri's eyes encompassed Roman and his brother. "If the smell of smoke hadn't woken me when it did, our whole place could have gone up!" Abruptly she felt the sting of tears. "Or was that your intention?"

Roman shook his head wearily. "Why don't you go home, Sheri? You've caused enough trouble here tonight. We don't need any more. So if you'll just get in...." He opened the car door.

"No!" She stood her ground. "And stop trying to make out I've something to answer for. You're the—"

"*Make out* you've something to answer for! That's a good one," he cut in harshly. "Our machinery's wrecked and I know who's responsible. You left proof this time, sweetheart!"

Books by Kerry Allyne

These books may be available at your local bookseller.

For a list of all titles currently available, send your name and address to:

Harlequin Reader Service
P.O. Box 52040, Phoenix, AZ 85072-2040
Canadian address: P.O. Box 2800, Postal Station A,
5170 Yonge St., Willowdale, Ont. M2N 5T5

Time
to Forget

Kerry Allyne

Harlequin Books

TORONTO • NEW YORK • LONDON
AMSTERDAM • PARIS • SYDNEY • HAMBURG
STOCKHOLM • ATHENS • TOKYO • MILAN

Original hardcover edition published in 1984
by Mills & Boon Limited

ISBN 0-373-02647-1

Harlequin Romance first edition October 1984

CHAPTER ONE

THE morning flight from Sydney to the central New South Wales town of Dubbo was an extremely anxious one for Sheridan Taylor. In fact, she had done little else but worry ever since her grandfather, Colin, had telephoned the previous afternoon with the mind-numbing news that Chris had been accidentally shot while out mending fences on the family sheep property, and that it was touch and go whether he would last the night.

Chris was Sheri's older brother, and although they hadn't seen very much of each other during the past nine years since their father's death—at the time Chris had opted, very much against his mother's wishes, to remain with his grandparents and work on the farm rather than return to the city with his mother and fourteen-year-old sister—the close bond that had always existed between them had not diminished during their resulting lengthy separations so that, in consequence, the shock of the previous day's tele-phoned information had made it seem as if it was only a week or so since she'd last spoken to him instead of nearly six months before.

Now, as the plane taxied to a standstill in front of the small terminal, Sheri quickly descended the steps to the tarmac below, her darkly fringed green eyes already scanning the crowd waiting outside the building, searching for the familiar figure of her grandfather. Not that she expected him to look quite the same as when she'd last seen him, of course. After all, the intervening years would no doubt have wrought changes in him just as they had in herself, but even so she still confidently expected to be able to recognise him at a glance.

However, after having crossed to the barrier and passed through the gateway without once having pinpointed his tall frame, she came to a halt with a slight frown putting twin creases between her arched brows, wondering if perhaps he hadn't altered more than she had anticipated, and beginning to re-check those present with a decidedly slower and more thorough gaze.

When this proved just as unrewarding, her somewhat perplexed frown grew a little deeper—since punctuality had always been one of her grandparent's strong points, she really couldn't imagine him being late on such a grave occasion—so she turned for the terminal building, supposing now that he must be inside. But just as she approached the doorway along with some of the other passengers from her flight, her attention was suddenly caught by a well-built man coming in the opposite direction, and the sight of him had her thoughts involuntarily flying off at a tangent.

Roman McNamara! His name sprang to mind swiftly, easily. And why wouldn't it? she went on to muse in a rather tart vein. When she'd lived on Ellimatta, her grandfather's property near Goonagulla—the small town approximately another hundred miles further west than her present destination—she had known him, or more especially his two younger brothers, almost as well as she had known her own, because the McNamara family lived next door. Much to her regret at times!

Land claims during the last century had begun something of a feud between their two families which had continued intermittently to the present day, and 'heri could well recall that as a result neither her nor her brother's days at school had been as carefree and uneventful as they could have been upon occasion. Not that Roman had become involved too often, she had to admit, her reverie continuing impulsively. Being Chris's senior by four years and her own by nine had always seemed to set him apart somehow from the rest of them, but only too well could she remember the scraps that had taken place between Chris and Morgan, and the seemingly never-ending teasing she had suffered at the hands of Hayden, the youngest.

With a dismissive shake of her head she returned to the present, and caught a sharp breath on seeing the catalyst for her musings only a yard or so away now, her glance becoming surreptitious as an almost hypnotic force had her scrutinising his commanding form.

He was tall and dark-haired, with rugged though undeniably attractive features that she was now of an age to more readily—even if grudgingly—appreciate, she noted with as much objectivity as possible. But when her gaze connected momentarily with his, she found his incredibly blue, thickly lashed eyes still holding the same lazily taunting light that had so disconcerted her as a teenager, and in a flurry of unaccountable and annoying self-consciousness she was only briefly aware of a straight masculine nose above a firmly shaped but sensuous mouth, and a strong-boned chin with just the hint of a cleft in its purposeful centre as she lowered her eyes rapidly and continued on towards the doorway.

'Sheri?'

The pleasantly deep half question, half statement, came from just behind her in a voice she remembered surprisingly well, and knowing she could hardly pretend not to have heard it, she ran slim fingers through her lightly waving, russet red hair in a discomfitingly nervous gesture and reluctantly about-faced with something of a sigh.

'Roman,' she acknowledged briefly, and shifted restively from one foot to the other—then promptly railed angrily at herself for the betraying action and squared her slender shoulders determinedly. Good lord, she was twenty-three years old, not some adolescent who needed to tread warily where any of his family were concerned!

To her embarrassment, Roman's lips twitched wryly in response to the action, as if he sensed only too well her desire to appear totally unaffected by their unexpected meeting, but to her relief he at least refrained from making any such comment. Instead, he merely surmised, 'You're looking for your grandfather, I expect.'

Sheri nodded quickly, glad to have her attention returned to her reason for being there. 'Yes. Yes, I am, as a matter of fact. Why, have you seen him?' she asked hopefully, again looking towards the milling figures still inside the terminal.

'Uh-uh, sorry.' He shook his head lazily. 'He's not here. You'll just have to accept my company, I'm afraid. I'm standing in for him.'

'For Grandpa?' She sought clarification in patent disbelief. Since when had a McNamara ever done anything for a Taylor, or a Taylor wanted them to, if it came to that? 'He didn't mention anything to me about it on the phone yesterday. In fact,' her gaze narrowed suspiciously, 'I distinctly remember him saying *he* would meet my plane this morning.'

Roman lifted one broad shoulder in an unconcerned
———. 'Mmm, but then he apparently wasn't feeling
    t last night, due no doubt to the excitement of
    ticipated return ... at long last.' With more

than a touch of sarcasm in his tone, Sheri realised in surprise, and indignation! What concern of his was the length of her absence? 'So as I had business of my own to attend to in Dubbo today, I offered to collect you on his behalf and thereby save him the added strain of a long drive.'

'I see,' she returned stiffly. But if he thought she was going to thank him for having relieved her of the necessity to make other transport arrangements, he was very much mistaken! She would rather have travelled in the often crowded station wagon the airline provided for its passengers going to and coming from Goonagulla. More importantly, however ... 'There's nothing seriously wrong with Grandpa, though, is there?'

'Not as far as I know. He's just not as young as he used to be, that's all, and of course, the shock of Chris's accident hasn't helped him, or your grandmother, much in that regard either.'

As well as being the more likely cause of his being off colour at the moment rather than her return! decided Sheri in silent resentment before finally voicing the question she was almost afraid to ask.

'And—and just how is Chris?' she faltered.

Roman expelled a heavy breath. 'According to the hospital, as well as can be expected. Which isn't very informative, I know, but ...' he half smiled reassuringly, 'at least he made it through the night, that's something.' His strong features sobered as he rubbed a hand around the back of his neck. 'They weren't at all sure he would yesterday when he first went in.'

'S-so Grandpa implied on the phone,' Sheri admitted on a slightly tremulous note, and averted her face. She didn't want to display any sign of weakness, of any kind, in front of this man of all people. And seeing the luggage from the plane now being taken into the building, she seized on the opportunity to distract his attention by exclaiming, 'Oh, there's my case. Shall we collect it and then we can get going? Naturally I'd like to see Chris as soon as possible, so if you could perhaps just drop me off at the hospital I won't keep you from your business any longer.' She began heading into the terminal even before she had finished speaking.

Roman's long legs kept pace with her easily. 'No sweat, it's already completed,' he drawled. 'In any case, Chris doesn't happen to be at the Base Hospital here in Dubbo. He's still in Goonagulla.'

Sheri came to a sudden halt. 'You mean, at the tiny District Hospital?' she gasped, knowing the facilities at Goonagulla were nowhere near as extensive as those at the Base. Then involuntarily, as the rueful thought flashed unbidden through her mind, 'Oh, won't Mother have something to say when she hears that!'

'Although only from a safe distance, presumably, since it's apparent that not even Chris's dire circumstances could have her overcoming her dislike of the west enough to make the journey with you,' he replied in a return to his sarcastic tone.

'Only because she happens to be on holiday in Fiji with some friends at the moment!' she defended angrily, loyally. Once again, how dared he comment, and especially so caustically, on her family's behaviour? All right, so her mother hadn't ever made a secret of her dissatisfaction with life in the bush, and sometimes maybe even with unnecessary corrosiveness, but that still didn't give him any right to cast aspersions! 'As it so happens, she still doesn't even know about the accident! When I tried to ring her at her hotel yesterday I was told she was on a trip to one of the outer islands for a few days where she couldn't be contacted, so all I could do was leave a message for her to phone me at Grandpa's as soon as she returned.'

His lips twisted mockingly. 'So that's why you've finally plucked up the courage to return, is it? Because your mother, who always did like to control her family's lives, wasn't there to make the decision for you and forbid it . . . as she usually does.'

For a time Sheri could only stare at him in mounting outrage, her green eyes glinting furiously. 'Oh? According to whom?' she grated between clenched teeth on eventually managing to regain some control over her flaring temper. The man's gall knew no bounds! But then what could she expect from a McNamara? she asked herself scornfully.

Totally unperturbed, Roman merely gave an indolent grin—a crooked shaping of his firmly moulded mouth that much to Sheri's vexation had her sucking in a dismayingly aware breath. 'Your family,' he relayed laconically.

'That's a lie, if ever I've heard one!' she denounced immediately, feeling on surer ground now. 'You forget, I knew from past experience that they wouldn't willingly tell you anything . . . about any one of us . . . and certainly not anything like that!'

'Mmm, but then *you* forget,' emphasising his words with a goading tap beneath her chin with a long forefinger, 'you haven't lived here for the past nine years, sweetheart. Haven't even visited during that time either, I might add . . . due no doubt to your mother's dictates,' he obviously couldn't resist adding, 'but that doesn't mean we've exactly been standing still all that time. In fact, you might be surprised at the changes that have taken place.'

'Including the Taylors supposedly discussing their most private matters with the McNamaras? That'll be the day!' she scoffed.

The latter remark he chose to ignore, electing to taunt instead, 'You're admitting I was correct, then?' And before she could even frame a suitable denial, let alone voice it, he indicated the luggage now ready for collection and went on to enquire, 'Which one's yours?'

'The two-tone blue,' she answered automatically, caught momentarily unawares, and handing over the baggage check she had been holding ready in her hand. Although recovery wasn't long in coming as she trailed after him towards the counter. 'And no, I was not making any such admission! Why would I when there's absolutely no truth it?'

Roman accepted her case from the attendant and began ushering her towards the entrance before replying. 'That's not the way Chris tells it, or Col, if it comes to that,' he asserted, holding the door open for her.

Passing in front of him, Sheri angled her head defiantly. 'And I still don't believe they've ever said anything of the sort! More especially not to you!'

'No?' One dark brow was raised expressively high. 'Then you're obviously forgetting again that many things aren't quite the same around Goonagulla as they were when you left, aren't you?'

He sounded so positive, so sure of himself—but then hadn't he always? she interposed with acid resentment—that now she really was finding doubts starting to surface. When all was said and done, and as she'd initially thought, just the fact that he was there in her grandparent's stead was some considerable departure from the norm, at least as she remembered it. Consequently, as they crossed the car park she found herself eyeing him a little less confidently.

'Such as?' she queried, but still with a note of disbelief in her voice all the same.

'For one, a cessation of the feud you appear so keen to continue,' he mocked.

Utter amazement, together with a tinge of inescapable chagrin, kept Shari silent as he saw her seated in a dark green station wagon and then deposited her luggage in the rear before continuing around to his own seat. The feud had been alive for so long now that she'd never really expected it to end, but if it had, why hadn't Chris ever mentioned it? And she said as much to Roman once he had taken his place beside her and set the vehicle in motion.

'Perhaps because you'd never shown any desire to even re-visit the property, he figured you wouldn't be interested,' was the suspiciously sardonic reply that had her flaring into protesting speech.

'Oh, of course he must have known I would have liked to have visited the property!'

'So why didn't you?' He slanted her a subtle glance. 'The decision not yours to make?'

Sheri drew an irate breath. He was back to that again, was he? Only this time she couldn't help recalling all those occasions during the last few years when she had intended paying her grandparents a visit, simply to have her mother present seemingly perfectly valid reasons why it would be more suitable for her to postpone her trip until some later date, and the niggling thought that by docilely accepting those suggestions she might have been allowing herself to be manipulated into doing precisely as her mother wanted—Heather Taylor had never disguised the antipathy she felt for her in-laws—now had her anger waning somewhat as it became tempered with inexorable feelings of doubt.

'I—well, whatever the reason, it's nothing to do with you!' she parried defensively, and received such an ironic look in return that an uncontrollable wave of

colour swept into her cheeks. 'An-anyway,' she rushed
on with a stammer, before Roman had an opportunity
to convert that knowing look into even more
discomfiting words, 'even if you and Chris have
decided to call it quits, it's impossible for me to
believe you've managed to persuade Grandpa into
doing the same.' As she recalled, the feud had been
almost a way of life for her grandfather.

A rueful smile of remembrance etched its way across
Roman's lips. 'Yes, well, I must admit there were
times when we thought we weren't going to succeed,
and even now he occasionally shows signs of wanting
to lapse back into his old ways, but on the whole it
seems to have worked quite satisfactorily . . . as well as
to everyone's advantage. There was certainly nothing
to be gained by continuing the feud, it always was
counter-productive, so we figured it was time to forget
our past differences and to let bygones be bygones.' A
lazily bantering gaze was flicked in her direction.
'Don't you agree?'

'I—I guess so,' she allowed, although not in a
particularly convincing fashion. The idea was still very
new to her, and the thought of being on friendly terms
with the man beside her suddenly seemed even more
disconcerting than opposing him.

'You don't sound very sure of that.'

Trust him to have noticed! 'So what did you expect
me to say? Something gushy?' Her defence mechanism
came into play once again.

'Not unless you feel a need for it,' he was quick to
retort, and equally satirical. 'Although a little more
enthusiasm sure wouldn't go amiss. As I said, for the
most part Col seems reconciled to the truce, but
unfortunately there's no guarantee that that state of
affairs would continue if he thought he had a willing
ally in his dear little granddaughter. So whether you

agree or not, sweetheart, I suggest you at least *appear* as if you do, otherwise Chris, for one, isn't likely to be exactly overjoyed if he finds when he recovers that you've undone all his efforts at reconciliation in the meantime.'

Ignoring everything else he said, Sheri clung to the first words of hope she had heard regarding her brother since learning of the accident. 'You really think he will recover, then?' she sought assurance anxiously.

Roman made an almost imperceptible flexing movement with one shoulder. 'Well . . . at the moment I guess about all we can do is hope, but what I do know is that if anyone can pull through this, Chris can. He's not only as strong as an ox . . .' his lips tilted crookedly, 'as Morgan could no doubt testify, but he's determined as well . . . and that's a combination which has a tremendous amount going for it in a situation like this.'

Oh, how she hoped so! 'You sound almost as if—as if you like him,' she commented, frowning a little. Although they had apparently worked together to bring the feud to a conclusion, she had only imagined it to have been as a matter of expediency.

'Why should that be so incredible?' He shrugged both shoulders this time. 'With our similar backgrounds, we have a lot in common.'

'I suppose so,' she conceded, albeit somewhat on the dubious side. 'It's just that I never thought I'd ever hear a McNamara say anything good about a Taylor, I guess.'

'Or vice versa?' he drawled mockingly.

The lazy glance which accompanied his words had her pulse racing strangely. 'No, definitely not that,' she averred on a jerky note, and looking away quickly, concentrated her attention on the passing countryside.

They had left the outskirts of Dubbo behind some time ago.

After the undulating hills of Sydney's lower north shore, where she and her mother lived, the black-earth plains of the central west now seemed even flatter than she remembered; the undeviating line of the highway, covered with its customary, shimmering heat haze, stretching before them as far as the eye could see.

Here and there small mobs of sheep could be seen grazing intermittently, their few visible numbers giving no indication of the huge flocks that abounded in an area which had long been renowned for its Merino stud farms. Rams bred in the district had been upgrading the nation's one hundred and fifty million strong sheep industry for more than a century.

However, as the miles flew past, Sheri's thoughts returned inevitably to her brother's plight once more and she turned back to her companion with something of a confused expression clouding her finely formed features.

'Why *wasn't* Chris taken to the Base in Dubbo, Roman? I thought it was a foregone conclusion that that's where he would be, with injuries as serious as his apparently are.'

'Yes, well . . .' He paused, releasing a long breath. 'He would have been if it had been at all possible, but unfortunately . . .' he halted momentarily again, eyeing her commiseratingly, 'the truth of the matter is, it was doubted he would survive the journey. We only just managed to get him to Goonagulla in time as it was, and although the doctor would have preferred to have been able to transfer him, in the end he had no option but to advise against it because he was of the opinion that Chris's condition was just too critical for him to be moved at all.'

'I see,' she nodded, swallowing painfully. Then, a

few taut minutes later, 'So j-just how did the accident happen?' Her grandfather's news had come as such a shock the day before that she had given no thought at the time to explanations.

'We don't know yet,' he advised with a brief shake of his head.

'You don't know?' she repeated in bewilderment. 'But surely Chris . . .'

'Chris was unconscious when he was found,' he cut in to inform her heavily. 'He wasn't in a position to tell anyone anything.'

'And since then?'

Roman raked a hand roughly through his hair. 'As far as I know he did come round some time during the night, but only briefly, I'm afraid, and apparently not sufficiently enough for him to even realise where he was, let alone be questioned.'

Sheri chewed at her lip miserably. It didn't sound very promising. 'Then whoever found him—Grandpa, I suppose—didn't he have any information to offer?'

'Actually, it wasn't Col who discovered him . . . I did,' Roman relayed in flat tones. 'But there was no one around that I could see when I got there.'

'You did make a search, though?' she put forward on a near accusing note.

Roman shot her a stare of hard-eyed intensity. 'No, I did not waste time making a bloody search! The plain facts were that your brother was bleeding to death before my eyes, so I happened to consider his interests would be better served by my getting him to a doctor as soon as possible than by scouting around looking for damned clues as to who had caused his condition! That could always be done later.'

'Yes, of—of course, I'm s-sorry,' she apologised despondently, close to tears. The strain of worrying about her brother's welfare, plus the inexplicably disturbing company she had so unexpectedly found herself in, was suddenly beginning to tell.

To her confusion, Roman reached across to brush his knuckles lightly against her cheek in a gently comforting gesture. 'So am I, sweetheart,' he half smiled ruefully. 'I guess the tension of waiting, and not knowing, must be getting to all of us, hmm?'

Sheri could only nod her agreement as his surprising understanding brought her nearer to crying than ever, and it was some time before she could trust herself to speak again in something approaching a steady voice. When she did, it was to query softly, 'Then how do *you* think it happened?'

'Since Chris hasn't an enemy in the world . . . not even a McNamara,' he grinned lazily, devastatingly from Sheri's point of view, 'at a guess I'd have to say it was probably caused by some idiot wanting to do a spot of shooting, but neither having the decency to ask permission to enter the property, nor having a clue what he was doing except to blaze away at the first thing that moved. And in view of the fact that whoever did it just left him, then I figure there's a distinct possibility they don't even know they've shot someone.' His demeanour turned to one of unmistakable disgust.

Sheri winced visibly. It was appalling to think her brother might lose his life owing to someone's abysmal carelessness, and they not even aware of it? Of course it wouldn't be the first time such an accident had occurred in the bush, but unfortunately that didn't make it any easier to contemplate.

'Do you think it could have been a local?' she asked next, frowning.

Roman lifted his shoulders noncommittally. 'I'd be surprised if it was. Most of them can handle a rifle and know what they're about when they go shooting. But at the same time ... who can say?' His lips twisted wryly. 'You can find irresponsibility anywhere.'

'I suppose so,' she acknowledged with a sigh, and in an effort to dispel the depressing thoughts the remark engendered, turned her attention to the view beyond her window once more.

To the left of the road a flock of galahs abruptly crossed her line of vision as they took to the air and wheeled overhead, displaying their rosy breasts which in the wild were closer to crimson than pink, and she watched them musingly until out of sight before resuming her survey of the roadside. Along the edges trailing vines of paddy-melons grew, their round fruit yellow in the autumn sunshine, but it was the small amounts of some fluffy white substance which was increasingly littering the sides of the highway that had her forehead puckering in puzzled concentration.

'What *is* all that white stuff?' she just had to enquire at last after exhausting all her own ideas as to what it might be. 'I don't remember ever seeing anything like that around here before.'

'No, you wouldn't have,' Roman half turned to advise with a smile. 'It only started about five or six years ago, but it's what a lot of people around these parts are going in for these days ... cotton.'

'Cotton?' Sheri's initial reaction was one of astonishment. She had always thought of Goonagulla as being an inveterate woolgrowing district. Her gaze returned to the edge of the roadway with renewed interest. 'Mmm, now you mention it, that's exactly what it does look like ... cottonwool balls,' she murmured meditatively. 'But where's it come from? I can't see it growing anywhere.'

'Because the farms along here don't border the highway, but you'll certainly see some before we reach town. This,' he indicated the white covering alongside the road, 'comes from the trucks taking the harvested cotton to the gin in town.'

'Goonagulla has a cotton gin?' Her eyes widened incredulously. 'Things *have* changed!'

Roman responded to her amazement with a lightly mocking laugh. 'I told you we hadn't been at a standstill since you left and that you might be surprised at the changes that had occurred.'

Might be! That was putting it mildly. 'And is it a very profitable crop?' Surely it would have to be to have had usually staunch woolgrowers switching to it.

'You could say that, I guess.'

Some veiled nuance in his tone had her gaze fastening to him watchfully. 'You've changed to cotton?' she partly guessed, partly quizzed.

'Uh-huh, in the main,' he drawled indolently. 'As have the Caldwells . . . among others.'

Her grandfather's two largest neighbouring properties, noted Sheri reflectively. The thought immediately giving rise to another. 'Not Grandpa too?' she gasped, unable to disguise her feelings of disbelief. She'd always thought of him as such a traditionalist.

'No, not Col.' Roman's white teeth gleamed in a wry grin.

Again, something in the way he'd spoken set her to thinking. 'But Chris wants to?' she hazarded this time.

'Maybe you'd better ask him that.'

Although his humorous expression hadn't altered, Sheri suspected that, since he hadn't been more expansive, that was probably as much as he intended to divulge on the subject and she would only be wasting her time by pursuing the issue. When he set his mind to something, as she knew from past experience, Roman McNamara wasn't a man to be easily swayed from his purpose. Besides, it would be a simple enough matter to discuss what was going on with her grandmother if, as appeared likely, her grandfather was opposed to the idea. She decided to return to the generalities of the topic instead.

'I'd have thought a crop like that would have needed more rain than you get out here, though.' It was neither a plentiful nor reliable commodity this far west.

'Well, yes and no,' Roman half laughed confusingly, then went on to elucidate. 'Mostly, cotton requires a very hot, dry atmosphere to grow really well—and that of course we have in abundance—but on the other hand, at certain times of the growing season it also needs extremely large amounts of water, so in order to combine the two we don't rely on rainfall, but use flood irrigation. There's a maze of water channels all through the area now and you'll start to see some of those too shortly.'

'And the water in these channels, where does it come from ... bores and storage tanks?' Those had been the main sources when she'd lived there.

'Sometimes, as a supplementary supply,' he confirmed. 'Although usually from the river, which in turn is replenished by releases from Burrendong Dam near Wellington.'

Sheri shook her head in an unbelieving gesture. The place certainly did sound as if it had changed radically during her absence. However, it still wasn't until they were closer to Goonagulla and had crossed one of the twenty- to thirty-feet-wide irrigation channels, and she actually saw for herself the huge tracts of land now being harvested of their white-bolled crop, that she could fully and finally grasp just how many alterations *had* taken place.

She knew they had just passed the turn-off to her grandfather's property, but if it hadn't been for the signpost at the side of the road she doubted she would

have recognised where they were, because so many of
the old familiar landmarks deemed to have disappeared. For where rough-barked collobah and mulga trees
had once sheltered grazing animals, they now only
provided windbreaks around vast and otherwise open
paddocks.

In one such field a trio of mechanical pickers could
be seen straddling the orderly rows of plants, their
barbed spindles plucking the cotton from the open
bolls, and blowers depositing it in large wire baskets at
the rear of the machines. However, it was towards the
middle of the paddock where a number of large
rectangular white objects with what appeared to be
black tops rested that Sheri's gaze kept returning, and
after studying them curiously for a few moments, as
well as noticing an even great number in the next field
they passed, she made her own deduction as to what
they were.

'They're containers for the harvested cotton, are
they? Those white boxes with black tops,' she
attempted to clarify.

Roman uttered a low chuckle and shook his head.
'No, sweetheart, that *is* the cotton, with a plastic
covering resting on it,' he explained. 'That's how the
seed cotton is transported to the gin. In compressed
modules, as they're called. There's about eight tonnes
of it in each of those.'

'I see,' she smiled at her own mistake. From a
distance they had looked like enormous foam
containers with lids. 'Then what happens to it?'

'At the gin, you mean?'

'Mmm,' she nodded. 'You often read about cotton
gins in books, but no one ever seems to get around to
actually explaining just exactly what does happen to
the product when it gets there.'

'Well, ginning is basically a process—automatic

these days, naturally—of separating the cotton fibre from the seed on which it grows by means of a series of circular saws rotating at high speed and drawing the cotton lint through fine combs, plus combing the fibre afterwards,' he advised efficiently.

So that was what happened. 'The seeds then being used for next season's planting, I presume?' Sheri hazarded next.

'Some are, after being treated, but the majority are crushed for oil. Like, vegetable oils for margarine and such.'

Sheri absorbed the information thoughtfully, although only transiently, for now they were approaching Goonagulla itself and she was more interested in noting whether the town had altered to the same degree as had the surrounding district.

The first big change she saw, of course, was the gin situated close to the highway, its yards containing some hundreds of modules waiting to be processed, and still more being offloaded from incoming semi-trailers. At the other end of the complex more transporters were being loaded with bales of already treated cotton so they could be forwarded to centralised storage sheds, so Roman informed her.

The town itself, she discovered, had not only improved during her absence but it had grown considerably too, although the lacy pepper trees which shaded both sides of the main street remained exactly as she remembered them, Sheri was glad to see. Some of the old buildings she had known were hardly recognisable now in their modernised forms, the new ones completely foreign, and where once she had recognised just about everyone in town, she now couldn't distinguish a solitary familiar face among those people busily making their way along the street.

Why, even the hospital wasn't the same any more,

she mused wonderingly, when Roman turned in at the gates and brought the station wagon to a halt a short distance from the front steps, because the bright new wing that had been added to the original structure had changed the whole aspect of the place here as well.

CHAPTER TWO

INSIDE the hospital a nurse was already at the reception desk, her round attractive face serious as she replied to some comment made by the elderly couple on the opposite side of the counter, and after her disappointment at not identifying anyone in town, it was almost with a sense of shock that Sheri realised she knew all three of them.

The nurse was Laurel Knox, a close friend from her very first days in primary school, and whose whole family she knew extremely well. Although it was to the white-haired couple that her gaze clung—her grandparents here, now!—and with a rather tearful smile beginning to illuminate her heart-shaped face she hurried forward to greet them eagerly. That was until she had almost reached them, whereupon their presence suddenly raised the haunting spectre of her worst fears and her steps slowed in dread.

'Oh, no! Chris isn't ...' she began in strangled, terrified accents.

'No, no, lass!' Colin Taylor hurriedly interrupted to put her mind at rest, correctly surmising what she was thinking. 'Quite the opposite really. Your grandmother and I are here because Laurel phoned us a while ago to tell us that Chris has finally regained consciousness.'

'Oh, thank God!' Sheri breathed fervently, and feeling suddenly weak with relief. 'That *is* good news, isn't it?'

'The best,' he agreed. 'Apart from hearing you intended to visit.'

'Yes, well . . .' She found herself flushing somewhat as she recalled Roman's previous criticism on that point, and knowing he could hear every word. 'I would have come before except that . . .'

'We know, darling, we know,' he broke in to dismiss her explanation with a shake of his head. 'Chris told us why you felt you couldn't.'

'Well, I'm here now,' she smiled mistily at both her grandparents. 'And it's lovely to see you again. I've missed you both.' She hugged and kissed each of them in turn.

'No more than we have you,' her grandmother, Beryl, returned fondly. 'Although at the moment I expect you're more anxious to see Chris.'

'Well, I . . .' Pausing, Sheri nodded a trifle apologetically before turning to her friend behind the counter. 'Is it possible?'

Laurel half smiled her permission. 'Only for a few minutes, though—I'm sorry. His condition is still critical, and as I was just telling your grandparents, unfortunately, even though he's regained consciousness, that doesn't by any means signify that, to coin a phrase, he's out of the wood yet,' she relayed with what sounded remarkably like a catch in her voice, and which had Sheri abruptly speculating whether the other girl's concern might possibly be more of a personal than professional nature. 'But if you'd like to come with me, I'll show you where he is.'

'Thank you,' Sheri acknowledged, and began moving after her friend—then sent her grandparents a surprised glance on discovering they weren't following also. 'Aren't you coming too?'

'No, dear, we've already seen him, just a little while before you arrived,' Beryl explained. 'Besides, it might prove too tiring for him if we all went in together.'

'Although I don't suppose it would hurt if Roman

accompanied you,' proposed Colin with an encompassing look for the younger man who had been standing by patiently while their reunion had taken place. 'I've no doubt he's as anxious to reassure himself about Chris's condition as any of us.' And to his neighbour directly, albeit somewhat gruffly, as if such words still came diffidently to his lips at times where his one-time adversary was concerned, 'I'm sorry, I haven't thanked you yet for collecting Sheri from the airport for us. It was very thoughtful of you to save me the journey.'

Roman accepted his gratitude with a wry inclination of his dark head. 'Think nothing of it,' he shrugged with negligent grace. 'As I said, I had business to attend to in Dubbo anyway, so it was no effort to call in at the airport on my way back. But you're right, I wouldn't mind seeing for myself that Chris is okay.'

'Well, since you were the one responsible for at least getting him here in time, I guess no one has a better right,' allowed Colin magnanimously.

Too magnanimously! railed Sheri impotently. Why, he was almost being treated as one of the family! And that she found an extremely unwelcome, not to say disturbing, contingency to consider.

'Oh, but Laurel perhaps might not think that's such a good idea,' she put forward as a result, hopefully obstructive.

To her disappointment, however, her friend disposed of the idea with unsuspecting helpfulness. 'No, it's quite all right. Dr Osborne did say, as it so happens, that provided the duration of the visit wasn't too long, two visitors at a time would be quite acceptable,' she smiled.

'Isn't that fortunate?' The taunting light in Roman's metallic blue eyes had never appeared more pronounced as he now joined the two girls and they began heading down the corridor, although his remark was clearly aimed at only one of them.

'Extraordinarily!' retorted Sheri in bittersweet accents, and she proceeded to ignore him as best she could until they reached the intensive care room where her brother was situated.

Here, after calling the junior nurse who was in attendance from the bedside, and repeating the request for them not to stay too long, Laurel left them alone.

At first Sheri could only stare about her in astonishment at the assorted equipment in the room—not as extensive as at the Base in Dubbo, maybe, but certainly more than she had ever imagined Goonagulla possessing—but the fact that most of it seemed to be connected to her brother's prone figure in some way left her feeling at something of a loss for words as she approached the bed, nor did Chris's appearance help her to find any when she reached it.

Attached to at least two intravenous drips, as well as a couple of monitoring, or life-saving machines—she didn't know which—he could have been a stranger, what with his normally tanned skin now hardly a shade darker than the pristine white sheet covering him, the gauntly drawn expression on his face, and the lustreless look in his hazel eyes as they focused on her drowsily.

'Oh, Chris,' she whispered on a quavering note, and had to bite hard at her lip to stop it trembling. She wasn't going to make him feel any better by crying all over him like a baby! she berated herself fiercely, but try as she might she couldn't force any other words past the swelling lump in her throat. All she could do, it seemed, was to clutch gently at the still fingers lying on the bed in front of her.

Perhaps because he sensed she was unable to continue, or maybe he just considered it was time for him to speak, but for whatever reason Sheri experienced a moment's gratitude—even if reluctant—when Roman stepped into the breach as he came to stand beside her.

'Hello, old son. How are you feeling?' he asked sympathetically of the younger man, and in a much more natural tone than she could ever have managed, Sheri had to admit.

Chris attempted a weakly wry smile and answered in one expressive word. 'Crook!'

'I'm not surprised, that bullet went perilously close to your heart ... as I'm sure you're now very much aware,' Roman's lips tilted lopsidedly, 'and you lost a hell of a lot of blood into the bargain.'

'Mmm, the reason for that, I suppose.' Chris eyed the drip feeding into his left forearm ironically. 'But I'm told I have you to thank for even being here at all.'

'All in a day's work,' Roman shrugged with a smile, making light of it. 'In any case, you were making the countryside look untidy just lying there.'

'Yeah, well ...' In what was obviously a supreme effort, Chris lifted his right hand slightly and held it out. 'Thanks anyway, mate. I won't be forgetting I owe you one all the same.'

Clasping the outstretched hand in a firm but careful handshake, Roman unexpectedly gave a rueful laugh. 'Then if you're so keen to remember it, I might just know a way you can square it,' he revealed drily.

'Trust a McNamara!' Indignation suddenly gave Sheri the power to regain her voice. 'Although you do at least intend to wait until he's out of hospital before demanding recompense, I hope!' she gibed, her gaze filled with contempt as she glared at the man next to her.

'Now that you come to mention it, not necessarily,

no,' he bent his head mockingly close to advise, and patently not one iota abashed by her outburst.

From the bed, meanwhile, Chris could only manage a gasped, 'Sheri!' in remonstrance, and she returned her attention to him contritely.

'I'm sorry,' she apologised immediately—for causing him any added distress, certainly not for any sentiments she'd expressed! she qualified silently—and sought to change the subject. 'However, any repayments aside,' she still couldn't resist flashing another derogatory glance upwards, 'I suppose you're wondering why Mother isn't here with me. Or did Grandpa explain?'

'No, in the short time he was here we didn't get . . . get around to discussing Mother,' he half smiled ruefully, his breathing starting to sound just a little laboured. 'So couldn't she face the . . . prospect of coming west again?'

'Chris!' It was his sister's turn to chide now, though rather more in puzzlement than condemnation. His reaction had been so similar to Roman's, they could almost have been carbon copies. Did they really know something she didn't? No, of course they didn't! she decided defiantly, and continued, 'You're not being fair. The reason she couldn't come with me is because she's not even in the country at the moment—she's on holiday in Fiji—but immediately she gets my message and rings me I know she'll waste no time at all in getting here.' When all was said and done, that *was* what any mother would do in such circumstances, wasn't it? Even reserved, undemonstrative ones like their own, surely!

'I shouldn't . . . bet on that . . . if I were you,' Chris recommended with an uncustomary sardonic twist to his pale lips, the pauses between his words noticeably lengthening now. 'Especially if . . . things aren't quite so . . . critical . . . when she phones.'

'Oh, naturally she ...' Roman's hand catching at her arm, and accompanied by a warning shake of his head, had Sheri breaking off in mid-sentence.

'I think it's time we were leaving,' he advocated meaningfully.

'Yes. Yes, of course,' she averred, her cheeks warming with a selfconscious heat. She shouldn't have needed him to point out the obvious. And to her brother, 'I'll be in to see you again tomorrow, okay?'

'I'll ... look forward ... to it, Sis,' he just managed to get out feebly before shifting his gaze to the man beside her. 'While *we* ... have things ... to discuss.'

'When you're ready, old son. It can keep for a while,' Roman told him casually as, with a friendly salute in farewell, he began escorting Sheri from the room.

'My, that was generous of you!' she promptly fired scornfully at him on reaching the corridor and seeing the nurse who had remained outside re-enter her brother's room. 'After all, seeing he was in no position to refuse it, I suppose you could have demanded your return favour right then and there, couldn't you?'

'Except that my last comment didn't happen to be a reference to any return favour, as Chris was well aware ... even if you weren't!' he retorted in a goading tone. 'Nevertheless, if you're really in the mood for sheeting home some truths, sweetheart, then try this one for size. At least whatever I had to say to him didn't nearly produce a relapse! Or perhaps you were too involved in trying to prove your point to notice?' One well-shaped brow quirked upwards to an unbearably sarcastic peak.

'Oh, you bastard!' Sheri choked anguishedly as all the worry and strain of the past hours found release at last in her escalating emotions, and her open hand cracked across his lean cheek with stinging effect before she could give a thought to what she was doing.

Roman's blue eyes blazed with a livid fire as he obviously fought for control in the tension-filled silence that followed her involuntary action. 'You bloody little shrew!' he denounced furiously. 'It would be no more than your just desserts if a man did . . .'

'Yes?' she dared to challenge recklessly, despite the fact that apprehension already had her heart pounding so heavily she thought it would burst.

'Give you reason to *really* complain, for a change!' he grated as he suddenly cupped her chin with a strong hand and tipped her startled face up to his.

Caught unawares, Sheri only had time to offer a muffled gasp of protest before his sensuous mouth clamped down over hers in a hard, punishing, but extremely thorough kiss that assaulted her senses like no other had ever done before, and left her feeling oddly dazed and weak at the knees when he finally condescended to free her.

'So in future, I might suggest you make certain of your facts before you give out with any further disparaging comments, sweetheart . . . for your sake, if no one else's!' Roman was back to his taunting, aggravating self again.

'Is that so?' Sheri seethed resentfully, her breasts heaving rapidly in time with her quickened breathing. 'Then it's a pity you don't believe in abiding by the same policy, isn't it? That way, I may have been spared all the unfounded criticisms and accusations *you've* been spouting all morning!'

'Save for the slight though not inconsiderable difference . . . as I'm sure you'll agree,' with a chafing smile that succeeded all too well in its intent, 'that *my* comments don't happen to have been unfounded,' he claimed with drawling arrogance. 'Or weren't you listening to *anything* Chris had to say?'

'Yes, I was listening!' she asserted hotly. He really was the most infuriating male it had ever been her misfortune to meet! 'Although I've noticed that neither of you has bothered to pay one scrap of attention to anything I've said!'

'Never mind, princess,' he consoled with dubious sincerity, 'I expect things will be different once you start . . .'

'Making my own decisions?' she surmised wrathfully in a moment's intuition.

Roman simply smiled—explicitly—and if she hadn't already learnt the folly of doing so, Sheri would have hit him. As it was, all she could do was curl her fingers tightly into her palms and content herself with a darkly smouldering green glare from beneath long lashes because she didn't trust herself to speak. Inwardly, she had plenty to say, though, as they continued on their way back to her grandparents.

So it was a decision he wanted, was it? Well, no doubt he would be very happy to know she had just made one! Because no matter what else she did during her stay in Goonagulla, she would find some way, *any* way, of taking him down a peg or two in return for all the things he'd said, and done, today! she vowed devoutly.

Not unnaturally, Chris's condition was the major topic of conversation in the Taylor household during the next few days, but as the week progressed and he continued to improve they were gradually able to lay their fears to rest and allow a more cheerful optimism to replace them. For a while it had been a close thing, but by the end of the first week it was obvious he was finally out of danger and that it

would only be a matter of time before he was
completely well again.

Visitors were also permitted to see him at any time
now, so when her grandfather proposed attending the
sheep sales in town one morning, Sheri took the
opportunity to drive in with him in the station ute.

'If I'm not back by the time you've finished, just
ring the saleyards and get them to put a call over the
loudspeaker for me, and I'll come back to collect you,'
Colin advised as he dropped Sheri off at the hospital.

'You don't have to do that,' she demurred, smiling
and shaking her head. 'They're only half a mile or so
away and it's a lovely day for walking.' The
temperature was pleasantly warm rather than hot, and
overhead the azure sky was cloudless. 'Besides, once
I'm on the road I'll probably see someone I know who
could give me a lift if I wanted one.' Although, as
she'd noted on her first day, there were a lot of new
faces in town now, she had also been pleased to realise
as the days passed that most of the older ones were
still there too.

'Well, if you change your mind, you know where I
am,' her grandfather accepted her decision compliantly
as he put the ute back into gear. 'Give my regards to
Chris and tell him I'll try and drop in for a few words
before we leave town.'

'Will do,' Sheri nodded, and with a brief wave as
her grandfather departed, she began mounting the
hospital steps.

Her brother's room—a different one from where she
had first seen him—was in the new wing with a view
of open bushland beyond the carefully tended gardens
which surrounded the building, and it was in this
direction that Chris was looking when she entered.

'Stop looking so wistful, you'll be back out there
soon enough,' she chided jokingly as she bent to kiss

him. 'Enjoy the rest while you're able.' She perched herself comfortably on the side of the bed. 'How are you feeling today, anyway?'

'Much the same as yesterday . . . still sore!' he half grinned ruefully.

Sheri's lips quirked in response, her head tilting to one side in a considering pose. 'Well, you certainly look a lot better,' she was happily able to report. He was nowhere near as pale and drawn now as on that first worrying day. Her green eyes slanted teasingly. 'Almost human, one might say.'

'Brat!' he laughed expressively, then grimaced and put a hand to his chest. 'Ouch! I don't think laughing's recommended. It hurts like hell.'

'Oh, I'm sorry, I should have realised.' Her forehead creased with concern. 'But I was just trying to cheer you up. You looked so glum when I came in.'

Chris's mouth curved wryly. 'I was mentally listing all the things I should be doing instead of lying here.'

'Mmm, that's what I thought,' Sheri nodded, part sympathetically, part admonishingly. 'At least, either that, or you were pining because you don't see as much of your favourite nurse now that she's on night duty,' she couldn't resist adding. A few cautious enquiries had brought to light the information that Laurel and Chris did indeed have a closer relationship than purely that of nurse and patient, just as she had suspected. Moreover, it apparently wasn't of a particularly recent origin either!

'Oh, we still manage to say a few words now and then,' he grinned unabashedly. 'But that reminds me . . .'

'It does me too,' Sheri broke in with a laugh, and continued before she forgot, 'Grandpa said to give you his regards, and that he'll try and call in to see you before we leave town. He's gone to the sales.' Her eyes widened enquiringly. 'Now what were you going to say?'

'About Laurel . . .'

'I'm all ears,' she inserted impishly, and received a heaved sigh of mock despair for her pains.

'I'll bet you are!' he retorted drily. 'But as sorry as I am to disappoint you, it wasn't really in connection with myself that I mentioned her.'

'Oh?' She glanced at him closely, her curiosity aroused. 'Then who?'

'Well, actually . . . it's you,' he revealed to her surprise, his lips twisting wryly. His pleasantly formed features suddenly assumed a more earnest mien. 'So do you think you could be serious for a minute, please, love?'

'Of course,' she agreed automatically, promptly, even as her puzzlement increased. What could he possibly want to discuss with her regarding Laurel that required such solemnity?

With a brief smile of gratitude for her ready acquiescence, Chris slowly began to enlighten her. 'Well, I'm not sure if you already know, but Laurel's young sister, Glynis, is to be one of the debs at the annual Debutantes' Ball this Saturday. It's still popular in the bush for young girls to attend coming-out balls,' he shrugged with somewhat rueful diffidence.

'So I gathered when I read about it in the local paper,' Sheri smiled. She suspected that deprecating hunching of his shoulders had been caused by the memory of the time when, as an eighteen-year-old, he himself had been roped in—extremely reluctantly, as she recalled—as the escort for the giggling daughter of a neighbouring family at a similar affair. 'And I did know Glynis was taking part, as it so happens. Laurel mentioned it one afternoon when I was talking to her.' Pausing, she gazed at her brother in a still confused manner. 'Although I'm still not quite certain what all this has to do with me.'

Chris didn't quite return her glance. 'I was supposed to be taking Laurel to the Ball, but now I can't, of course, so I was—er—wondering if you'd go instead . . . to—umm—represent the family, as it were,' he all but mumbled.

'To represent the . . .! Why, Christopher Taylor, you sneaky devil!' she charged with a delighted laugh as the import of his words sank in. 'You really are serious about the girl, aren't you?'

'Mmm, I guess I must be,' he owned drily. Or was it sheepishly? chuckled Sheri to herself. 'But will you go?'

'Oh, naturally I will if you want me to! Although I'll have to buy something in town to wear. I didn't bring a formal dress with me.'

'You can charge it up to me, if you like,' he offered.

Sheri shook her head quickly. 'Don't be an idiot, of course I won't. I could do with a new evening gown, in any case.' Her expression sobered a little. 'Of more interest, though . . . when do you plan to tell Mother of your intentions?'

'Yeah, that's going to be a hard one.' Chris rubbed his fingers across his forehead in a rueful gesture. 'She's always made it very plain that she's never given up hope of persuading—or should that be browbeating?' he inserted on an eloquent note, 'me into moving to the city with both of you, so when she discovers I'm not only considering marriage but that neither Laurel nor I have the slightest desire to begin our life together anywhere but in Goonagulla, God only knows what her reaction is likely to be!' He expelled a deep breath. 'So for now, perhaps you'd better just keep the information to yourself. I'll tell her about it when I get out of here.'

'Which should be ... when?' His first suggestion she was only too willing to comply with. Their mother could be decidedly cutting when matters went against her wishes!

'According to Doc this morning, probably not for another week,' his reply was delivered in such a long-suffering tone that it brought a smile to his sister's face. 'By which time Mother might even have managed to leave Fiji ... do you think?' His brows arched sardonically.

'I—well, it wasn't her fault she couldn't get a seat on a flight prior to her previously scheduled one,' Sheri felt obliged to justify, even if uncomfortably, and not really with a great deal of conviction. She had to confess her parent's excuse for not leaving the islands immediately had sounded a little thin to her too when Heather had rung a couple of days ago in reply to her daughter's original message, and been told that, by then, her son had finally been taken off the danger list. 'As a matter of fact,' she continued, looking down at the patterned bedspread and tracing the design with a slim forefinger, 'she phoned again last night.'

'To convey her best wishes for my speedy recovery, no doubt.'

At that, Sheri did lift her head, her eyes widening in sudden shock. Now that he'd mentioned it, she realised she couldn't remember her mother having expressed any such sentiments at all, either time she had been in contact. Not that she could admit as much to Chris, though.

'Naturally,' she lied as convincingly as possible. 'As well as to advise that she would be in touch again as soon as she returned home.'

'Whereupon, with any luck, she will learn that I've recovered completely, more or less, thereby precluding any necessity on her part to venture this far west again,' he predicted not altogether facetiously.

Since her once confident ability to forecast her mother's reaction had proved just about non-existent during the past week, in all truth Sheri didn't feel able to gainsay his supposition, and yet she still couldn't quite bring herself to completely agree with it either. That would be tantamount to owning that Chris—and more vexingly, Roman!—had been correct in their reading of the matter, while she had been totally, discomfitingly, wrong.

Instead, she temporised wryly, 'Would you really prefer it otherwise?'

Chris acknowledged the perception of her remark with a significant grin. 'You could have a point there,' he allowed humorously. 'I must say it's always far less of a strain when Mother's at a distance, and with the news I have to impart . . .' His eyes rolled upwards expressively.

'There'll be fireworks galore!'

'You're such a comforting little soul!' he retorted in satirically bantering tones. 'Are you sure you don't have someone else you could visit so you can make their life miserable instead of mine?'

'What, and leave you all on your own? I wouldn't think of it!' Pearly white teeth glistened in a teasing smile.

'Mmm, that's what I was afraid of,' he returned drily, and laughed at the retaliatory glance of feigned menace he received as a result. The accompanying movement, even though slight, nevertheless had him pulling a remorseful face again, and as his eyes continued to survey his sister's animated expression, his own demeanour remained thoughtful. 'Seriously, though, love,' he went on musingly, 'haven't you ever considered—er—breaking the maternal ties too, as it

were, and coming back here to live? I mean, you're old
enough to make your own decisions these days, and I
know you never wanted to leave either originally.'
Halting, a slightly whimsical light entered his eyes.
'Or is this Todd I kept hearing about from Mother the
last time I was in Sydney—the one she says you're
almost engaged to—the major force holding you in the
city now?'

Sheri gave a despairing shake of her head. 'Oh, I'm
not almost engaged to him!' she denied with a half
sigh, half grimace. 'Mother just seems so set on me
marrying him that I'm beginning to think she's
embarrassed by the fact that she has a twenty-three-
year-old daughter who's still single.'

'Better not to marry at all than live to regret it,'
were her brother's thoughts on the matter. 'Although
I was also informed he's extremely eligible.'

'In a monetary sense, I suppose he is,' she
conceded, shrugging. 'And that's an important factor
in Mother's estimation.'

'I can imagine,' Chris averred implicitly. 'But more
importantly, how do you feel about the guy?'

With another vague raising of her shoulders, Sheri
began picking absently at her skirt. 'To be quite
honest, I'm not sure really,' she confessed finally, a
trifle selfconsciously. It was the first time she had ever
discussed Todd with anyone but her mother, and
those times had usually taken the form of her mother
lecturing her on what she would be missing if she
didn't marry her latest escort. 'I know we do have a lot
in common, and he's certainly pleasant enough, but at
the same time he doesn't – he doesn't exactly . . .'

'Turn you on either?' her brother had no
reservations in concluding for her.

'Something like that, I guess,' she half smiled wryly.

'Then give him a miss, love, no matter what Mother

says,' he recommended without hesitation. 'You're the one who'd have to live with him, not her, and quite frankly, as far as I'm concerned you've got too damned much going for you to have to settle for second best.'

A light flush lent her cheeks a rosy glow. 'That wouldn't be brotherly bias speaking, by any chance, would it?' she laughed.

Chris wouldn't admit to anything of the kind, but contended, 'I still know a good sort when I see one, even if she is my sister. As has also been noted in certain other quarters too, I might add.' His eyes twinkled brightly.

'Oh?' Sheri looked at him humorously, sceptically, askance. 'What other quarters?'

'You'd probably be surprised,' with a secretive smile, 'but I still get to hear things, you know, even though I am confined to this damned bed.'

'From whom? Grandpa?' she mocked.

'As a matter of fact, no,' he took obvious pleasure in denying. 'I'll have you realise I've had quite a few other visitors apart from the family this last couple of days.'

She wasn't surprised. Her brother had always been popular—with both sexes. But with her thoughts diverted, she couldn't help grimacing, 'Including Roman McNamara?'

'Uh-huh,' he confirmed lazily. 'But what made you single him out?'

'Probably because I just don't happen to like him,' she had no compunction in divulging.

Chris's brows peaked graphically. 'Why on earth not? You'd have to be in a minority among the females in this town with that attitude,' he relayed on a dry note. Then, with his hazel gaze narrowing, 'Or are you still harbouring grudges because of that stupid feud, even though you promised not to do anything to revive it?'

The feud be damned! Sheri had enough grievances from the present to fuel her antagonism. She didn't need to look to the past for any. 'No, I'm not harbouring any grudges against him,' she denied. If it came to that, she didn't really have any against Roman from the past. Her problems had mainly been with his youngest brother in those days. 'I simply find his particular brand of assured superiority utterly in-sufferable, if you must know!' The corners of her mobile mouth tilted whimsically. 'So how about we discuss something else, hmm?'

Chris seemed quite amenable. 'Then to return to a question you didn't get around to answering . . . Have you ever considered moving back here, Sis?'

In response she partly hunched one slender shoulder in a noncommittal movement. 'Oh, I used to wish I could, but you become accustomed to living in the city after a while,' she smiled faintly. 'Besides, Mother would probably never speak to me again if I even remotely mentioned such an idea. I mean, even last night on the phone, she made no bones about how annoyed she was because I intended to stay here for the whole four weeks of my holidays now that I've returned. She was of the opinion that two would have been quite sufficient, and then I could—should!—have spent the remainder with Todd.'

'You let her play on your sympathies, you know,' he admonished gently.

It was something Sheri herself had at times suspected her mother of doing. 'Maybe so, but what else can I do? You know how opposed she's always been to my coming back here . . . that's why I've never come,' she sighed. 'She makes me feel I'm somehow being disloyal just by raising the subject.'

'Precisely! And by the sound of it, if you're not careful she'll make you feel just as guilty if you don't allow her to push you into marriage with this Todd whatever his name is!'

'Bradbury,' she supplied mechanically.

'Of the newspaper Bradburys?'

'He's the younger son,' she nodded.

Her brother's lips curled in wry derision. 'No wonder Mother would like to see the knot tied as soon as possible! She'd consider that some feather in her cap to have her daughter married into that family, wouldn't she?'

Sheri didn't immediately answer but chewed at her lip contemplatively. Once again Chris was putting into words what she had only suspected. 'You really think that's the only reason she's so keen on the match?' she frowned.

'Well, since you're obviously nowhere near as enthusiastic, you could hardly say it was *your* happiness she was considering, could you?'

'Perhaps she thinks . . .'

'What?' he cut her off summarily. 'That if she harps on the subject long enough you'll let her make this decision for you too, just like all the rest?'

His words were too reminiscent of someone else's and she took no less exception to them now than she had then. 'That's not true!' she flared defensively. 'I do make my own decisions.'

'Which just happen to always coincide with what Mother wants!' Chris eyed her ironically.

'They do not!'

'So tell me one of any importance that hasn't!'

For a moment she could only look at him doubtfully, but then her glance turned triumphant. 'My decision to spend the whole of my holidays here,' she announced on an almost relieved note.

Her brother didn't appear particularly convinced, however. 'And is that a sign of things to come, or just because she wasn't there to veto it?'

Again, as someone else had charged! Abruptly Sheri's feeling of success died even more speedily than it had arisen and she returned his slightly cynical gaze dispiritedly. 'You think I'm weak-willed, don't you?' she sighed.

'No, love, anything but, actually,' he disclaimed with as emphatic a shake of his head as he could manage. 'You're just too soft-hearted for your own good, that's all. And knowing it, Mother unfortunately isn't above taking advantage of the fact.'

Sheri moved her head perplexedly. 'I've never heard you talk like this about her before.'

'So when have we ever had an opportunity to talk like this before?' he promptly countered in sardonic tones. 'If you recall, we never seem to manage to have *any* time alone together when I visit Sydney.'

'You think Mother's deliberately tried to prevent us talking?' Her eyes widened in amazement.

'I don't *think*, I *know*,' he corrected, drily expressive. 'She's always been determined that you, at least, should never return to Goonagulla, and she as good as told me when she first took you to Sydney with her that she'd do anything possible to see I didn't get a chance to persuade you to go against her wishes too.' His mouth quirked ruefully. 'And Mother, I'm sorry to say, is nothing if not unrelenting in her desire to control her family's lives.'

Sheri frowned reflectively. Now where had she heard that before? Oh, yes, how could she have forgotten! 'So Roman claimed the first day I arrived,' she disclosed, reluctantly.

'It doesn't surprise me, Roman's nobody's fool. He can also remember what Mother was like when she lived here.' He paused—almost indecisively, his sister thought—then continued in a lighter voice, 'And while we're on the subject of our neighbour . . .'

'I wasn't aware we were!' she retorted with a grimace. 'In any event, he's *your* neighbour, not mine!' For preference, she wanted no connection with him at all.

'Yes—well . . .' Chris smiled at her in a noticeably sheepish manner, 'I just thought it may have been— umm—as good a time as any to mention . . .'

'Mmm . . .?' she inserted shortly, a suspicious frown beginning to mark her forehead.

'Who I've arranged to escort you to the Ball,' he concluded hastily, but with an encouraging smile.

'How could you have?' The unexpectedness of his reply distracted her for a minute and had her staring at him in surprise. 'You didn't even know I'd be going until a few minutes ago!'

'No, but as I thought it was more than likely you would agree—well, I certainly hoped you would—it seemed only reasonable to arrange an escort too,' he relayed brightly.

Suddenly everything began to add up and, wanting none of it, Sheri glared at her brother direfully. 'Oh, no, you don't, Christopher Taylor!' she smouldered. 'You're not partnering me with Roman McNamara just because the two of you are so pally these days! I'd sooner go on my own! And if you dare to tell me that's what you've so conveniently arranged, then so help me, I'll put a bullet in you myself!'

Chris's expression became ruefully apologetic. 'In that case, I guess I'd better ask Col to ensure you don't get your hands on any of the rifles, hadn't I?'

It was as good as a confirmation. As she knew he'd intended it to be. 'Yes, you had!' she retorted resolutely. 'Because my answer's still no! I want nothing whatsoever to do with him.' A chance thought came to mind. 'Why can't you ask Grandma and Grandpa to go instead?'

'Because I've already arranged with Roman for the two of you to go together!'

'In other words, it's all right for you to decide where I'm to go, and with whom, but not for Mother, is that it?' Her emerald eyes rounded facetiously.

'No, of course that isn't it!' he denied the suggestion a trifle vexedly. 'It just never occurred to me that you'd find the idea so objectionable. Besides, I thought you might enjoy an evening out.'

A wry curve caught at her lips. 'Yes, well, thanks for the thought. With anyone else I probably would! But as it stands there's no way . . .'

'Not even as a favour to me?' Chris interposed on a persuasive note. 'I mean, when all's said and done, the man *did* save my life, so would it really be asking too much for you to show at least some appreciation on my behalf for his effort?'

Sheri looked away discomfitedly. By asking it as a favour to himself he made it very hard for her to refuse, but at the same time . . . 'I was under the impression he'd already thought of a way for you to do that! Or does he now expect every member of the family to make a contribution as well?' she couldn't help but gibe scornfully.

'For crying out loud, Sheri, *I* asked you to do me the favour, not Roman!' he part exclaimed, part laughed in a somewhat bemused fashion. 'And for your information, that token repayment he mentioned—the thought of which seems to have so nettled you, although lord knows why—was just that, a *token* of what I owe him, and not only that but a request I would willingly have complied with anyway!'

'Such as?' she grimaced, still not altogether believing.

'Now that, my love, is something between Roman and myself,' Chris grinned uninformatively.

'Because anyone else might not think it quite so insignificant?'

Chris didn't reply. He merely gave a disbelieving shake of his head and relaxed back against his pillows to fix her with a meditative gaze. 'You know, for the life of me I can't understand just how you've managed to form such a dislike for Roman in so short a time,' he mused idly. 'There wouldn't be more to this than you're telling, would there?'

'No, of course not!' she repudiated swiftly, if a little selfconsciously as she remembered the perturbing effect Roman's kiss had engendered, and certainly not as firmly as she would have liked. Sliding off the bed, she moved across to the window before turning to look at him again and shrug, 'What else could there be?'

'You tell me,' he invited. 'But you did agree not to revive the feud, and yet every time Roman's name is mentioned you immediately start bristling as if you had a score to settle.'

To Sheri's dismay she felt her cheeks flush warmly. 'I—I told you why. Because he rubs me up the wrong way, that's all,' she attempted to defend herself flusteredly. 'In any case, I only agreed to help maintain the truce . . . not to—to personally associate with Roman McNamara!'

'One way of ensuring the former could be by doing the latter, you know,' he put in slyly.

She pulled a disgruntled face. 'Except I wasn't intending to take my participation to any such lengths!'

'Such lengths? Attending one Ball!' He raised his left brow mockingly.

She tried another tack. 'Anyway, I doubt Roman's any more enamoured of the prospect than I am.' He'd certainly found enough fault with her the day she had arrived! 'And I'm sure he . . .'

On seeing his glance flicker past her momentarily, she halted, and flashing a hasty look over one shoulder found Roman's commanding figure to be leaning negligently against the door frame behind her. Just how long he had been there she had no way of knowing, and as a result, as well as to her distinct irritation, she acknowledged his ensuing greeting with some disconcertion.

'You look considerably improved since I saw you last,' Roman then went on to remark to Chris as he crossed to the foot of the bed where he bent to casually rest bronzed and sinewed forearms on the food trolley. 'Some opposition getting the adrenaline pumping, hmm?' An amused gaze was slanted in Sheri's direction and then returned to the bed's occupant.

'You're not wrong,' Chris grinned wryly, and had his sister including them both in a seething glance. The knowing, and almost conspiratorial, character of their smiles aggravated intensely!

'Now—you were saying . . .?' Roman caught her off guard by abruptly turning to prompt in a lazy drawl.

For a moment she couldn't remember, but when she did, it was to propose with dulcet hopefulness, 'I was saying, with regard to your escorting me to the Ball . . . that I was sure you must have someone else in mind you would rather take.'

'No, I don't think so,' he replied blandly. Too blandly, in Sheri's estimation, and arousing the suspicion that he was only going along with the idea because he'd already deduced she would be opposed to it! 'And especially not when it's such a golden opportunity to present a completely united front to Col.'

Sheri gave a caustic half laugh. 'Why would you

need to? From what I've seen, he already treats you as if you were part of the family!' With her lips pressing together in patent dissatisfaction, 'What more do you want from him?'

'For preference, an agreement to at least be willing to *discuss* our experimenting with cotton,' came the startling insertion from Chris, which had her looking from one to the other of them in surprise before finally concentrating on the man at the end of the bed.

'This is all your doing, I suppose?' she immediately accused.

The unmistakable irony in Roman's return glance told all too clearly just how illogical her reaction had been, even without his wryly drawled, 'Now why the hell should I give a damn whether the Taylors grow cotton or wool?'

A mortifying heat swept upwards to her hairline. 'N-no, I guess not. I—I'm sorry,' she just managed to force out. Apologising to this man didn't come easily. For more than one reason, she rapidly switched her attention to her brother.

'So you *are* interested in growing cotton,' she deduced. Just as she had thought that first day, only circumstances had dismissed the matter from her mind and she hadn't got around to discussing it with her grandmother as she'd intended.

'Uh-huh!' Chris nodded decisively. 'But how did you apparently know? Don't tell me Col's said something to you about it?'

'No, Grandpa mostly seems reluctant to even mention the word unless he can't avoid it,' she advised on a wry note. 'I just guessed you may have been as a result of something Roman said on the trip here, only he wouldn't give a definite answer when I asked him,' shooting a mildly peeved look towards the end of the bed.

'Probably didn't want to become involved in what is essentially a family dispute,' speculated Chris, exchanging a grin with his neighbour.

Then it was a shame he didn't feel the same where other members of the family were concerned too! Sheri gibed acrimoniously to herself. Aloud, she frowned, 'Not that I can see what any of this has to do with my *perhaps*,' stressed pointedly, 'attending a Ball.'

'Well, apart from anything else, it would tend to show a united front, as Roman said,' Chris reminded her. 'While at the same time providing you with the means to maybe drop a few suggestions in Col's ear yourself regarding the benefits to be accrued by our diversifying with cotton.' He eyed her hopefully, coaxingly.

'You mean you want me to help you put your ideas across to Grandpa?' Her wing-shaped brows arched in unison.

'In a word ... yes,' he owned drily. 'If you will.' He paused, an oblique half smile tilting his lips. 'After all, every little bit counts when you're dealing with someone as obstinate as Col can be, and it's not as if I'm suggesting anything that's likely to be detrimental to him, or the property.'

Knowing her brother, and his feelings for Ellimatta, Sheri didn't suppose it would be, but neither did she want to become involved with Roman McNamara. 'Well, maybe Grandpa's opposed to the scheme because he can't afford it,' she evaded. 'From what I've seen, I should imagine it's rather a costly business to venture into from the word go.'

'True,' Chris agreed. 'But the rewards are worth the outlay, and the property isn't exactly down to its last dollar ... as you should be aware, since it also supports Mother, and to some degree yourself, in very comfortable style.'

'Yes, I know, but—but what makes you think Grandpa will listen to anything I have to say on the matter, when he won't even discuss it with you?' she parried now on a flurried note, sensing him about to systematically destroy her objections one by one.

'Because he already knows my views on the subject, whereas yours will be completely new to him, but if they should just happen to coincide—and since there's a distinct possibility he'll be more prepared to talk to you owing to your having been absent for so long— well, who knows what his reaction might be? So how about it—as a favour—hmm?' he blatantly played on her loyalty in a disarming fashion.

Sheri sighed helplessly, but, still loath to commit herself, didn't immediately reply. Then, before she could, Roman joined in with a goading assumption of his own.

'It's too difficult a decision to make on your own, is it?'

As before, he was implying because her mother usually made them for her! she supposed wrathfully, and in an impetuous moment's desire for reprisal, very rapidly proved to herself, at least, that when it really came down to it she was as capable of making decisions as anyone else. If it was mockery he wanted, then that was exactly what he would get! she decided tartly.

'Not in the slightest,' she denied his claim at last with equally taunting overtones. 'I was merely thinking over what Chris said, because you do realise, don't you, that our spending one evening together at a Ball is hardly likely to convince Grandpa I've had sufficient time to learn anything of consequence to the feasibility of growing any crop. We'd have to spend much more time together than that.' So much so, in fact, now that she had decided—however precipi-

tately—on her course of retaliation, that if she had her
way he would be heartily sick and tired of her presence
by the time her stay in Goonagulla was concluded! she
vowed balefully. Then they'd see who felt like being
sardonic, wouldn't they?

'Mmm, I had thought that myself if it's to have the
desired impression on Col,' Chris concurred happily
with her last proposal. 'So you really have decided to
help, then, after all?'

She nodded quickly. Before she had time to change
her mind? the rueful musing promptly followed when
a covert, sidelong glance showed Roman to be
watching her with a discomfitingly shrewd light in the
depths of his remarkably blue eyes, and not with just
the gratitude that was apparent in her brother's. With
a challenging lift of her head she faced him directly.

'Satisfied?' she dared to mock.

His firmly moulded mouth shaped into a lazily
captivating smile that had Sheri's breath unexpectedly
catching in her throat. 'How could I fail to be?' he
drawled slowly. 'It would appear I've not only
acquired an extremely attractive partner for the Ball,
but also a . . . willing companion as well.'

The slight but eloquent hesitation before his last
words caused Sheri a few momentary doubts, but she
dismissed them blithely. Naturally she was willing.
She was very willing! she smiled with inward
satisfaction. Although for entirely different reasons
than he surmised, of course.

CHAPTER THREE

'I SUPPOSE it was all Chris's idea, was it?' growled Colin Taylor somewhat exasperatedly as he drove Sheri back to the homestead after having collected her at the hospital as promised.

'My going to the Deb Ball with Roman, you mean?' she sounded cautiously. Surprisingly, in view of his previous attitude towards his neighbour, her grandfather hadn't seemed particularly in favour of the arrangement when told about it.

He nodded shortly.

'I guess so,' she shrugged. There was certainly no reason for the idea to have originated with Roman. 'He just asked me if I would go because he couldn't, and then arranged for Roman to be my escort since he was apparently already planning to attend owing to his being a cousin of the Knoxes. What's wrong with that?' A lot from her standpoint, of course, but she could hardly say so now without ruining her brother's hopes. 'After all, the feud is supposed to be laid to rest now, isn't it?'

'So what's that got to do with anything?' He flashed her a sour glance. 'Feud or not, Roman McNamara would still be dangerous company for any woman! Or is it just that undoubtedly virile physical attraction of his which had you agreeing to accompany him in the first place?' He spared her another glowering, probing look.

Recovering from her surprise caused by his totally unanticipated objection, Sheri only just managed to stop herself uttering a vehement disclaimer in time.

She did still have a part to play. 'Well, he *is* good-looking, and I must admit he does have a certain way with him,' she declared instead with a selfconsciousness that wasn't entirely feigned.

'As well as quite a reputation for wanting to remain unattached!'

A circumstance which didn't cause her any bother in the least. In view of what she had in mind, it was probably all to the good, in fact, 'Oh, well, it will be a novel experience, anyway,' she predicted nonchalantly.

'Huh!' he snorted, unimpressed. 'And what about Nerissa Whitelaw? Or is she just a thing of the past now too? Just like all the others he's ever escorted!'

Nerissa Whitelaw! Was she his current girl-friend? Well, well, fancy that! Sheri could remember her from her schooldays, and although the other girl was some years older than herself, there had never been any love lost between them. As she recalled, Nerissa also had a way with her—more often than not a spiteful, vindictive way—and the thought that her plan to commandeer Roman's time would no doubt peeve the older girl as well did add just a little more spice to the idea, Sheri had to admit.

In consequence, she wasn't above replying to her grandfather with a pertly smug, 'I guess she must be.'

'You know about her, then, apparently.'

'Not that she'd been dating Roman,' she owned indifferently. 'But I certainly know *her*.'

'Hmm . . .!' Colin's lips levelled in evident dissatisfaction. 'And it doesn't bother you to think that's all you'll no doubt be to him in a couple of months too . . . just another name!'

Provided it was one he remembered with annoyance she would be more than content, mused Sheri pleasurably, hiding a smile at her grandfather's straitlaced attitude. It was the last thing she had anticipated.

'Well, that remains to be seen, I guess, doesn't it?' she countered.

'Maybe,' he allowed, though without any sign of conviction. 'Nonetheless, in the meantime I'll have you know there's no way you'll be attending that Ball on your own with him!' he continued in a resolute voice. 'Your grandmother and I will be there as well to ensure it's only a novel experience, not a regrettable one. Even if you're misguided enough to want to chance your reputation with that one . . . I'm not!'

Sheri blinked incredulously, unable to believe she'd heard right. 'Grandpa, I'm twenty-three years old! I don't need chaperoning!' she partly expostulated, partly laughed in her disbelief. 'Good lord, we're only going to a glorified dance, not an orgy! What on earth do you think is likely to happen?'

'Who knows? Anything seems acceptable these days!' he alleged curtly. 'And there's still the journey to and from the homestead to consider.'

'So?' She cast him an amused glance.

'So on second thoughts, your grandmother and I will drive you in and bring you home too. If you're determined to go with him, you can meet him there.' His decision was arbitrarily made.

Although the arrangement would have suited Sheri just fine, there were other reasons why she felt the need to protest. For one thing, it would be as good as telling Roman she was expecting him to make a play for her, when she actually wanted nothing of the kind.

'Grandpa, that's taking it a little too far!' she exclaimed. 'It would be unbearably humiliating having to tell him that, and besides, I—I want to go with him.' Well, she would if she really was as interested in him as she was supposed to be, wouldn't she?

Colin exhaled irritably. 'I don't like it,' he grunted.

'Mmm, I sort of got the feeling you didn't,' she half smiled drily. 'But he's not the first man I've ever been out with, you know.'

'He's the first one while you're under my protection,' he promptly retorted in gruff tones. 'So let's have no more talk about it, hmm? Just because Chris was thoughtless enough to arrange it, neither of you need think I'm going to be as accommodating. Someone has to keep a discerning head on their shoulders.'

Sheri sighed ruefully. This was going to be harder than Chris had envisaged. She tried another angle.

'But Roman *was* instrumental in getting Chris to hospital,' she reminded him persuasively. 'And you definitely didn't appear to have any reservations about him collecting me from the airport. In fact, as I recall, at the time you said you were grateful for his help.'

'That was different!' he maintained in a slightly uncomfortable, blustering manner. 'I also said I didn't want to discuss it any more, didn't I?'

A wish Sheri would probably have respected if it hadn't been for her brother. If she was to help him at all—as well as put her own plan into action—she had to at least partially overcome her grandparent's objections. Meanwhile, there was another avenue she hadn't yet tried.

'What about Mother, though?' she put forward in a more hopeful vein.

'Well, what about her?' Her grandfather's iron grey brows rose steeply. 'Since she hasn't even seen fit to return to the country as yet, you're surely not suggesting I should ring her to seek her thoughts on the matter, are you?'

Actually, nothing had been further from Sheri's mind. In fact, considering how her mother felt about her relationship with Todd, it was also the last thing she wanted mentioned to her parent!

'No, of course not,' she denied hastily. 'I simply meant that as Mother's due to return to Sydney on Saturday, it's more than likely she'll phone that evening, and if you and Grandma also go to the Ball she could be worried if there's no one at the homestead to receive her call.'

'Then seeing Goonagulla's a manual exchange she can have it put through to Chris at the hospital, can't she!' It was an exasperated statement rather than a question.

'Somehow I doubt Mother would think of that.' Sheri's lips curved ruefully. Heather Taylor always expected people to be waiting on her calls, not to have to search them out.

'Then that's her problem!' he contended on a terse note. Ever since those first days when his daughter-in-law had shown herself to be totally uncaring of anyone's wishes but her own a state of barely suppressed antipathy had existed between the two of them. 'Perhaps she should have made arrangements to fly home earlier—I don't doubt she could have if she'd really made an effort to—but as it is, she'll just have to ring again on Sunday, won't she? Because there's no "if" about it ... your grandmother and I will definitely be going to the Ball.'

Which seemed to settle that! 'Although you're not going to insist I drive in with you, are you?' Sheri tried for at least one concession.

'It would save him time,' Colin parried. 'After all, we're further from town than he is.'

'Not by much if he comes via the back road. There are gates there, remember?'

'So there are,' he nodded.

'Well?' she quizzed when it became obvious he wasn't about to add anything further.

With a long-suffering look for her persistence, he finally relented, albeit not with particularly good grace. 'Oh, all right, if that's what you want. But he'd better bring you straight home afterwards!'

'Will he have any choice, since you'll no doubt ensure you tail him the whole way?' She eyed him sardonically.

He didn't deny it. He just smiled, complacently. 'At least it will remind him just whose granddaughter he's escorting!'

To Sheri's relief her grandmother had no such misgivings about her intended partner for the Ball, and although Colin seemed somewhat disgruntled by his wife's obvious support for the idea, he said nothing further on the subject and by the time lunch was concluded appeared to have become resigned to the situation.

'So how about we go for a ride this afternoon?' he suggested to Sheri in his more customary placid manner as she completed the last of the drying up and draped the tea towel she'd been using over a rack beside the sink. 'I'd like to check the fencing in Beefwood Paddock. We've had a few roos in there of late, and it was due to their having brought some of the fence down that Chris was out there that day.'

'So he said,' Sheri relayed with a nod, and cast him a drily hopeful glance. 'By ride, I take it you do mean on a bike?' As it had been nine years since she'd last been on a horse, she had strongly suspected that if she attempted that kind of riding she would more than likely spend a good deal of her vacation feeling extremely sore and sorry for herself, so to date she had made certain that on those occasions when she had accompanied her grandfather out on the property it had been by the less punishing mode of travel of trail

bike. Her father had first taught her to ride one many
years past.

'I do, as it so happens,' Colin endorsed with a smile.
'So hurry up and get changed and I'll meet you down
at the shed.'

Re-emerging from her room a few minutes later
after exchanging the dress and sandals she had worn
that morning for jeans, shirt, and an old pair of her
grandmother's short-sided riding boots, Sheri re-
trieved her brother's wide-brimmed and flat-crowned
hat from a peg beside the back door and clapped it on
to her head as she hurried across the yard to where her
grandfather waited for her.

The Honda she used was her brother's too, the
engine flaring into life at the first kick, and as Colin's
did the same she gestured with her head for him to
lead off, then followed him out of the yard.

For the most part Ellimatta consisted of flat, black-
soil plains, watered by a couple of creeks and
billabongs when they were flowing—which they
weren't at present—but more often than not by a
number of earth dams and artesian bores. However,
because it was so flat and relatively free from rocks it
made for easy riding, and despite the stops they made
at the two dams they passed to ensure no stock had
become bogged around the water's edge, it wasn't long
before they reached the Beefwood Paddock—so named
because of the profusion of beefwood trees it
contained; the colour of the freshly cut heartwood of
which resembled raw beef—and closing the wooden
gate behind them they started following the fence side
by side where it was possible.

'There was a large group of roos dozing in the shade
way over on the right back there. Did you see them?'
Sheri called over the now slightly more muted noise of
their engines.

Her grandfather nodded. 'I also saw you having a bit of a race with a couple of emus,' he chuckled back. 'You watch you don't hit a stump or something. One in hospital is enough!'

'Don't worry, I wasn't trying that heard.' And as yet another of the long-legged birds crossed their path and then darted back into the undergrowth again, 'They've sure got a turn of speed, though, haven't they?'

Colin nodded again, and for a mile or so they rode along silently, inspecting the fence as they went. Towards their boundary with Castlewood—the McNamaras' property—they began to notice some slackness in the two top single strands of wire—below it was steel-meshed—and a yard or two before they reached the junction where the two fences met they found a section bent low to the ground and hopelessly tangled.

Judging by the flattened vegetation on either side it appeared probable that both kangaroos and emus had decided it was a likely place to cross from one paddock to the other, but as Sheri and her grandfather drew to a halt so that he might start effecting repairs—he never went anywhere without a box of tools strapped to the rear of his bike—Sheri's gaze was irresistibly drawn to the unimpeded view on the far side of the boundary where, in staggered formation, half a dozen mechanical cotton pickers were methodically divesting a huge paddock of its crop.

'Well, that really is broadacre farming on a grand scale, isn't it?' the exclamation was forced from her involuntarily. The area under cultivation stretched just about as far as the eye could see in any direction.

'Mmm, Roman never does do anything by halves,' her grandfather replied somewhat wryly, bending to inspect the damaged fence more closely.

Sheri brought her gaze back to her own surroundings meditatively. 'And is this where—where Chris's accident happened?'

'No, not this side,' he answered, coming upright now and gesturing towards the north. 'Along the other . . .' Abruptly he came to a stop, his lips levelling to a disgruntled line. 'Now what the hell's he doing here? As if he hasn't caused me enough worry for one day!'

'Who?' she queried with a frown as she followed the direction of his glance towards a clump of trees a little further along the boundary.

'Who do you think?' came the sardonic retort, which was almost immediately followed by the rather accusing-sounding question, 'Did you know he was going to be here?'

At last able to discern two drill-clad figures standing next to a white ute on the opposite side of the fence, Sheri looked nearly as displeased as her grandfather for a moment. She hadn't anticipated seeing Roman again that day either! His companion she didn't recognise at all. She shook her head quickly.

'No! Why would I?' she countered. 'Besides, you were the one who suggested we come out this way.'

Colin mumbled something like, 'A suggestion I think I'm beginning to regret,' on a dry note under his breath and sent her a wily look from beneath lowered brows. 'Then since you didn't think to see him, you won't be wanting to talk to him, will you?'

Fortunately she didn't have to answer that one. The matter was taken out of her hands. 'I don't think the choice is going to be mine to make. They already seem to be walking this way. I guess they must have heard the bikes,' she deduced in what she trusted was a suitably pleased tone. After all, she was supposed to give the impression of enjoying the man's company, wasn't she?

Her grandfather uttered a resigned sigh. 'Well, if we

must, let's get the pleasantries over and done with,
then. Just you remember, though, I came out here
to work, not for some social get-together,' he
complained in a gruff voice as he started for the
boundary.

Clasping her hat in one hand, Sheri gazed at his
departing figure affectionately as she combed her
fingers through her flattened hair—he really wasn't
the grouch he often liked to make out he was—and
then hurried after him. They reached the corner post
at about the same time as Roman and his companion
did, and Sheri launched into speech immediately.

'Well, this *is* a pleasant surprise! I didn't expect to
see you again today,' she warbled sweetly at the taller
of the two men opposite her, and fluttering her
extravagantly long lashes for good measure. 'What
brings you out this way?'

If he was surprised by her sudden display of
effusive amiability, Roman didn't show it by even the
faintest change of expression—somewhat to Sheri's
disappointment. He merely returned her slightly
facetious regard with a steadily assessing gaze of his
own and, in reply to her query, said laconically,
'Work.'

'Although had he known you were going to be here,
the propelling force would doubtless have been
pleasure, I'm sure,' put in his companion gallantly on
noting the winsome glance she was casting at the
younger man beside him.

'Oh, unquestionably,' Roman smiled lazily, bringing
a disconcerting rush of colour to Sheri's creamily
smooth cheeks. She hadn't missed that driest of
inflections in his voice, even if the others had.
'However . . .' he continued in the same tone, 'after
that opening, perhaps you two had better meet. Sheri
Taylor—Max Dawson,' he supplied briefly. And to

Max, 'You already know Col, Sheri's grandfather, of course?'

'Yes, we've met in town a few times,' Max acknowledged genially, smiling his response to Colin's ensuing greeting. He was a stocky, round-faced, and ruddy-cheeked man in his late forties with an easygoing, casual manner that belied an extremely shrewd business brain. 'And I'm pleased to meet you too, Sheri.' He paused, his expression sympathetic. 'I was sorry to hear about your brother, though. But I hear he's on the mend now.'

'Thank goodness,' she both smiled and nodded with feeling. 'But Dawson . . .?' Her head tilted to one side in slightly frowning contemplation. 'I can't seem to recall the name. Have you always lived in the district?'

'No, I'm one of the new breed,' he laughed. 'Cotton's my principal game.'

'Oh, you're another grower, are you?'

'No, Max is a contractor,' Roman inserted. 'Those are his machines out there.'

'I see,' she nodded, her eyes straying of their own volition to the pickers in the paddock behind him as they continued inexorably from row to row. 'They're certainly efficient, aren't they?'

'Too right!' Max agreed earnestly. 'Especially in the hands of my girls.'

Sheri swung her gaze back to him in surprise. 'Do you mean girls are driving those machines?' Normally one tended to associate men only with such occupations.

'Uh-huh,' he smiled to see her obvious astonishment. 'During the three months the harvest's on we need about a third more workers, and a lot of those hired are female. It might be hard, dusty work, involving long hours at times, but they seem to figure the money's worth it, and they drive a variety of the machinery—not only the harvesters—as well as working in the gin.' He started to laugh. 'Some even reckon they do it just in order to get to the picking party at the end of the season.'

'It's a good one, I gather?' she surmised humorously.

'It sure is!' His endorsement was expressively voiced. 'You want to get Roman to bring you and then you'll be able to see for yourself.'

Not that she expected to still be in Goonagulla by then, but ... 'I might just do that,' she averred brightly, and proceeded to bat her eyelids shyly in his companion's direction. 'As long as Roman's willing, that is.'

For his part, Roman dipped his head mockingly. 'It will be my pleasure,' he drawled.

Beside her, Sheri's grandfather exhaled heavily, and gave her a dour look. 'I thought you only intended to stay four weeks,' he commented suspiciously.

Without quite looking at him, she hunched slim shoulders in an offhand gesture. 'I—well, perhaps I'll find a reason to stay a little longer,' accompanied by another brief but significant glance across the fence. 'You wouldn't object, would you?'

'That all depends on the reason you decide to stay,' he came close to snapping. 'But what about your work? Don't you have to get back for that?'

Naturally she did. Although after her last remark, she could hardly admit as much. As well as that, she reminded herself, no matter how mean she was beginning to feel by deceiving her grandparents in such a fashion—her pleasure at the thought of annoying Roman notwithstanding—there was still her brother to consider. She *was* going to have to spend a reasonable amount of time with Roman if she was to convince her grandfather she knew enough about the subject of cotton to prevail upon him to at least discuss it with Chris.

'Oh, I expect something could be arranged,' she therefore replied airily. 'My boss is pretty understanding most times.'

'That's fortunate,' he muttered on a caustically heaved note, and started shuffling his feet in a show of impatience.

'Yes, isn't it?' Sheri agreed innocently, but sensing his increasing desire to leave, she continued hastily before he had a chance to voice his wishes. 'It will give me that much longer to renew acquaintances and catch up on all that's been happening since I left. And talking of change . . .' her wide-spaced green eyes sought Roman's again, 'I wouldn't have recognised Castlewood, it's altered so much.' Indicating the paddock behind him with a nod of her head, 'Don't you raise any livestock at all nowadays?'

A heavily muscled shoulder was lifted impassively. 'Not as many as we used to, although we haven't entirely forsaken our beginnings . . . as some claim.' A chafing smile tugged at the corners of his firmly cut mouth as his gaze rested momentarily, implicitly, on her grandfather. 'There's still a couple of thousand head in the back paddocks.'

'Yes—well—before you become too involved in his enterprises . . .' Colin interposed sardonically, eyeing his granddaughter with an exasperated glance, and starting to make movements towards leaving in earnest now.

'Okay, I know, you want to get on with your fencing,' she acknowledged with a laugh, judging his indulgence to be nearing its end. When all was said and done, she was only supposed to help channel his thoughts in a new direction, not to aggravate him. That emotion, if she had her way, was solely to be aroused in Roman! 'Well, let's get to it, then.' She linked her arm with her grandfather's companionably, and smiled across the fence as she added her own farewells after he had finished his. Then, having turned to leave, she flicked the taller of the two men a bashfully coquettish look over her shoulder. 'Will you—umm—be in town tomorrow, by any chance?' she quizzed in her most demure manner.

Roman folded his arms across his broad chest and fixed her with a watchful, narrowed blue gaze. 'Why?' he countered unhelpfully.

Only just managing to remember he was the one who was supposed to be irritated by her ploy, not herself, Sheri gritted her teeth and valiantly tried to stop her smile from slipping. 'Well, as I have to go in to buy a dress for the Ball, as well as to see Chris, I just thought that if you were in town too . . .' she drew a deep breath, 'then we might have lunch together. Provided you have nothing else planned, of course,' she added swiftly in an endeavour to alleviate her own embarrassment in case he refused.

'I expect he has, though,' put in her grandfather—hopefully, it sounded to her. 'This is a busy time for cotton growers, you know.'

'Even so, I'd still make time if I received a proposal like that from such an attractive young lady,' said Max jovially.

Roman simply half smiled crookedly. 'In that case, I guess it would be ungentlemanly of me to do otherwise, then, wouldn't it?'

'Not at all,' asserted Colin generously. Of course he was willing to be understanding to a fault now! his granddaughter observed ruefully. 'Sheri knows that sometimes it's just not feasible for a farmer to alter his schedule, and I'm sure she wouldn't want to put you to any trouble.'

'No, naturally not,' Roman acceded, but so ironically that Sheri felt a swift spurt of pleasure surge through her, knowing he was aware that was exactly what her intention had been—and also aware that, in the circumstances, there was very little he could do about it! 'Fortunately, however, in this instance my arrangements don't happen to be that inflexible, so there's no problem.' One dark brow peaked quizzically above dusky-framed eyes as they came to rest on Sheri's artlessly cultivated expression. 'We'll meet at the hospital, then, shall we? At about ... twelve-thirty?'

'Yes, that will do fine. I'll look forward to it.' She deliberately made her eyes sparkle provocatively at him.

'The feeling's mutual,' Roman drawled in a lazily mocking tone, raising a finger to the flat brim of his bush hat. 'You're sure you wouldn't like me to drive you in to town too?'

He was being sarcastic, she knew, but having scored one success, she wasn't above trying for another. 'Well, now that you mention it ...' she pondered dulcetly.

'There's no need! I can take you in, the same as I did today,' her grandfather offered promptly, resuming his more familiar obstructive manner again.

Damn! Why couldn't she have been satisfied with one victory for the day? She could hardly turn round now and say she'd meant to drive herself in all along, and if she wasn't careful, now that she had unthinkingly presented him with the opportunity, there was always the chance her grandfather might just feel inclined to invite himself into joining them for lunch in order to keep them both under surveillance!

'Oh, but you won't want to be away from the property that long, will you?' she queried anxiously. 'I mean, I was thinking of going in first thing in the morning, and—and you were only saying the other day how the work's been piling up what with all this running back and forth to town.'

Colin smiled wryly, as if fully conscious of the reasoning behind her concern. 'No worries, I'm not intending to stay in town any longer than I absolutely have to in order to conduct some unfinished business,' he said drily. 'I was only planning to drive you in . . . nothing else. Your grandmother can drive you home again once she's seen Chris in the afternoon.'

'I see,' Sheri nodded, her relief tinged with a certain amount of selfconsciousness which she attempted to dispel by rapidly returning her attention to Roman and pouting with assumed disappointment. 'In that case, it seems I won't have to take you up on your kind offer, after all. I shall just have to meet you at the hospital as previously suggested.'

'So it would appear,' he acceded blandly. 'Perhaps some other time.'

'I shall do my best to arrange it,' she threatened rather than promised as a parting shot before heading off with her grandfather.

Finally able to get on with what he wanted to do, Colin set about repairing the fence, but in the middle of re-straining the top wire he stopped for a moment to eye his granddaughter speculatively.

'Are you sure you know what you're doing?' he questioned with a frown.

In the act of tying the bottom mesh more firmly to the fence post, Sheri looked up in surprise. 'I should do—I did this sort of thing often enough as a kid. Besides, you'd tell me if I wasn't, wouldn't you?' she grinned.

He shook his head faintly. 'I meant, with regard to Roman,' he explained in a heavy voice.

'Oh, that,' she smiled contentedly. 'Yes, I'm sure I know what I'm doing. Very sure!'

'He—he attracts you that much?' roughly.

The thought of plaguing him certainly did! 'I guess he must.'

Her grandfather drew in a deep breath. 'More than this Todd your mother's been telling us about?'

'Differently,' she parried, shrugging.

'In what way?' He paused, his lips twisting contritely. 'Or am I beginning to sound like an inquisitor?'

'Only a little,' she half laughed, but purposely refraining from answering his first question.

'Hmm ...' He went back to straining the wire thoughtfully for a minute. Then, in an outburst he was obviously unable to withhold, 'Well, I'm still against you becoming involved with him! And what's more, I don't intend for him to be taking any liberties with any granddaughter of mine either, I can tell you!'

Suppressing a smile at his quaint phrasing, Sheri adopted a placatory manner. 'Grandpa, you're working yourself up over nothing,' she said soothingly. 'What makes you think he's likely to?' She certainly had no intention of allowing anything of the kind to occur.

'He's got the reputation, hasn't he?'

Her eyes widened teasingly. 'You mean, for taking liberties too?' she gasped in mock horror.

'I mean, don't make the mistake of taking him too lightly!' he retorted on an exasperated note. 'He's not a man to be underrated, and particularly not by any sensible female!'

'All right, I'll be careful,' she acquiesced fondly, knowing he only had her best interests at heart, and then promptly put his warning out of her mind as she concentrated on what she was doing.

CHAPTER FOUR

TRUE to his word, her grandfather didn't stay around after driving Sheri in to Goonagulla the following morning, but almost immediately set off again about his own business, leaving her to make the rounds of all the dress shops in town on her own in search of a suitable gown to wear to the Ball.

However, despite the town's relatively small size and the limited amount of boutiques, it still took her considerably longer to find what she wanted than it would have done in the city, owing to the number of friends and acquaintances she met in the street with whom she stopped to chat. Even the girl who sold her the gown she finally selected—Robyn Bedford—was a former school friend, and it seemed only natural for them to make the most of the opportunity to fill each other in on what they had been doing since Sheri left.

'Mmm, that does suit you,' the blonde-headed Robyn now claimed enthusiastically as Sheri took one last considering look in the mirror at the creation she had chosen before donning her street clothes again. It was a slim-fitting, tiered gown of frilled gold and green organza with a diagonal neckline that left one honey-tinted shoulder completely bare, and which moulded itself sensationally to her shapely, curving outline. 'You'll be the envy of every other female there . . . including me,' she went on with a laugh. 'So who's the lucky feller?'

Sheri started to grimace and then thought better of it. 'Roman McNamara,' she revealed offhandedly.

'You're kidding!' Robyn's blue eyes rounded in

amazement. 'We'll be sharing a table, then. Although I was certain he'd be . . .' With her cheeks colouring warmly she came to an abrupt halt and hastily began ushering Sheri towards the changing room. 'If you'd like to pass it out when you've taken it off, I'll wrap it for you while you're getting dressed,' she offered flusteredly.

'There's no rush. I was going to ask you to keep it for me until after lunch, anyway,' Sheri said negligently, but declining to actually enter the small cubicle. It had required very little effort to guess the reason for both her friend's suddenly embarrassed expression and her rapid change of topic, and tilting her head to one side she eyed the other girl humorously as she hazarded, 'You were certain Roman would be . . . taking Nerissa Whitelaw, perhaps?'

'Well—yes,' admitted Robyn, looking even more stunned. 'B-but how did you know?'

'Oh, word gets around,' Sheri shrugged carelessly, and finally consented to enter the changing room. 'So what's she like these days?'

'Who . . . Nerissa?' Robyn's voice carried over the partition separating them. 'Do you mean with regard to looks, or personality?'

Sheri pressed her lips together and answered quickly, 'Both.' Not that she cared, of course. It was just that the information might come in handy some time.

'Oh, much the same as she's always been,' Robyn divulged with a half laugh, half grimace, as she took the gown now handed out to her. The older girl had never endeared herself to any of the younger ones at school. She had treated them all as if they were only there to do her bidding. 'You know Nerissa. She may look small and terribly delicate, but actually she's as strong as they come and has an iron will to boot!' She paused reflectively. 'Of course that air of fragility and the helplessly feminine manner she somehow manages to convey do still tend to bring out everyone's pampering, protective instincts, though.'

'Including Roman's?' queried Sheri sardonically, shrugging into the clover-coloured, short-sleeved dress she had worn that morning.

In the act of wrapping the organza gown, Robyn hunched one shoulder somewhat vaguely. 'Particularly Roman's, I would have said. At least ... un-until now,' she faltered, beginning to sound bemused again.

'I see.' Sheri pulled a caustic moue at the mirror as she flicked her waving, russet hair into place. 'Because she's his—*was* his,' she corrected swiftly, remembering her plan of action, 'latest girl-friend?' After all, if it was acceptable for Roman to apparently ignore the existence of his girl-friend when it suited him, why should she have any qualms about doing the same? Especially when it afforded the two-fold opportunity to turn the tables on both him and the unlikeable Nerissa!

'I—I suppose so,' Robyn conceded confusedly. She was clearly finding it difficult to come to terms with the sudden change of events.

'But what's this about our sharing a table?' Sheri frowned on leaving the cubicle, recalling the earlier remark. 'Who's your partner, then?'

'Hayden,' wryly.

'McNamara?' Sheri gasped—unnecessarily, since he was the only one of that name in town.

'Uh-huh,' confirmed Robyn in an amused tone at the look of astonishment now on her friend's face. 'As a matter of fact, we're getting engaged when the harvest's finished.'

Good lord! Thoughtful, uncomplicated Robyn to marry aggravating, tormenting Hayden! Who would have believed it? Recovering, Sheri offered warmly, 'Congratulations! I hope you'll be very happy.'

'Thank you, we hope so too,' Robyn acknowledged with a shy smile. Then, in a slightly teasing voice, 'But what about you and Roman?'

'I don't follow you,' Sheri frowned warily. 'What about us?'

'Well, considering Nerissa's sudden and apparent—umm—departure from the scene, plus no love ever having been lost between your two families before, I figure there would have to have been one hell of a magnetic attraction—on both your parts—to have you two willingly spending time together, and particularly on such a short re-acquaintance! So how about you do a bit of explaining now, eh?'

'Oh, you know how it is,' Sheri smiled coyly, certainly not averse to furthering the other girl's assumption, although at the same time not wanting to put it into so many words. 'What with a truce having been called to the feud, other avenues are open for exploration now and, as I'm sure you'll agree, they always were an exceptionally good-looking family.' A glance at the clock on the wall behind the counter and she gave a tinkling laugh. 'One of whom, however, could be just a little annoyed if I don't hurry, though! I'm supposed to be meeting Roman for lunch in ten minutes,' she leant forward conspiratorially to impart, 'and I still haven't been to see Chris yet.'

'Oh!' Robyn's fair brows flew high in appreciative response on hearing of the luncheon appointment—as Sheri had meant them to do. Farmers didn't often take time out in the middle of the day for such entertainment! 'And—and how is Chris?' she obviously felt compelled to enquire rather than put forward the questions of a more personal nature she was just as patently longing to ask. 'Progressing well?'

'Mmm, improving daily, I'm glad to say,' Sheri told her. 'But I must rush. I don't want to keep Roman waiting.' With another arch smile she began making for the door. 'I'll pay for and pick my dress up later, okay?'

'When you can tell me all about your lunch,' Robyn nodded, clearly intending to discover whatever she could on the matter, as soon as she could.

Sheri just smiled, blandly, and continued on her way. All depending on exactly how Roman felt about having been forced—no, persuaded had a better ring to it—into this meeting, there very well might not be anything she would *care* to disclose afterwards! Still, one could always hope, she grinned incorrigibly to herself as she hurried across the street.

It was twenty-five past twelve by the time she reached the hospital, and although she had half suspected Roman himself would deliberately be late in retaliation for her having so arbitrarily commandeered both his time and person, conversely it didn't altogether surprise her to find him already in Chris's room awaiting her arrival. That had been another partly formed suspicion. His demanding to know of Chris just what the hell was going on!

'Good afternoon!' She encompassed them both with her vivaciously smiled greeting as she crossed to her brother's side. 'I'm sorry I couldn't get here sooner,' she apologised, bending to kiss his cheek, 'but it's taken me until now to find a suitable gown for the Ball. I didn't want to disgrace our family, or my escort,' with a chaffing glance through her lashes at Roman, 'by wearing just any old thing.'

Chris ran a hand through his more brown than red hair and eyed her askance. 'No one thought you would,' he denied wryly. 'The same as no one thought you'd be proposing meetings for lunch either.'

Ah, so it had been pointed out who had made the suggestion, had it? 'Just doing my best for the cause,' she shrugged blithely. 'Why, have you been receiving complaints regarding my efforts?' Another taunting sidelong glance found its way to Roman's tweed-jacketed and cream moleskin-clad length.

The indolent blue gaze she received in return had her feeling strangely uneasy, though, and she swung her attention back to her brother hastily in time to see him shake his head and advise in ironic tones, 'No, there's been no complaints. Although at the same time, no one asked you to act as if you've just found the love of your life either, you know.'

Sheri's lips twitched uncontrollably. So Roman was already beginning to think she was throwing herself too wholeheartedly into her part, did he? And to think she'd only just started! she chuckled delightedly to herself. With a widening smile playing about her shapely mouth she sank on to the edge of Chris's bed and, supporting herself on her hands as she leant back slightly, raised one shoulder in a carefully negligent gesture.

'Don't worry, I'm not,' she said mockingly, and certainly not for her brother's edification only. 'If I had, my attitude would be quite different, I can assure you.' Crossing slender, curving legs, she began swinging her raised foot. 'However, if you're now regretting having involved me ...'

'That isn't what I was saying!' Chris protested a trifle exasperatedly.

'No, but perhaps Roman ...' Limpid green eyes were fixed in a demurely downcast direction.

'Uh-uh! Don't alter anything on my account,' came the immediate veto, followed by the drawling, goading addition, 'Or maybe it's really on your own you're apparently now having second thoughts. Is that it?'

Sheri's head lifted quickly. 'I don't know what you mean,' she partly stared, partly frowned at him.

'I mean ... cold feet, backing out ... call it what you like,' he enlightened her sardonically.

'Cold feet about what?' interrupted Chris with expressively arching brows. 'She only has to act friendly.'

'Quite so,' endorsed Sheri with determined nonchalance, refusing to surrender to a challenging gaze of metallic blue. Naturally there were degrees of friendliness, but all of a sudden she knew without a doubt that Roman was all too aware there was far more to her extravagant brand of affability than merely helping her brother, and the knowledge had her breathing deepening somewhat apprehensively. Not that she allowed any such nervousness to show, of course, as she went on to quiz brightly, 'What possible reason could I have for getting cold feet?'

'Apparently none,' Roman smiled slowly, and had Sheri's pulse pounding raggedly, disconcertingly, in response to the lopsided tilting of his sensuous mouth. 'Which I'm sure must be very reassuring for Chris to hear.'

As swiftly as that initial unbidden sense of awareness had assailed her, Sheri now found herself filled with misgiving, and as much as anything it was the look of satisfaction that had accompanied Roman's last lazily voiced remark that had caused the rapid reversal. For some unknown reason, it made her feel as if she had just been outmanoeuvred, and yet she couldn't quite see how. When all was said and done, in view of her intention, she wasn't the one likely to want to back out ... was she?

'I still can't see why you would have thought it might be otherwise,' Chris inserted, looking perplexedly from one to the other of them. 'Especially since it was Sheri who suggested the two of you have lunch together today.'

'Mmm, that *was* a piece of quick thinking on her part,' Roman granted drily.

Sheri smiled sweetly. She thought she could detect just a hint of lingering vexation in his tone. 'Not that it's succeeded in feeding the inner me yet, though,' she couldn't resist reminding him pointedly.

'My apologies!' He promptly inclined his head mockingly, exaggeratedly low, and offered his arm. 'I didn't realise you were so anxious for us to leave. I thought you might have wanted a few words with Chris.'

'Oh, I do,' she verified on a purring note as she rose, smiling, from the bed to link her own arm lightly with his. 'But it can wait until later . . . when we'll be able to talk privately.'

Apart from a slight narrowing of measuring eyes and the brief tensing of the sinewed forearm beneath her fingers, Roman gave no outward acknowledgement of her purposely snubbing remark, but her brother did.

'Sheri!' he remonstrated with a frown, casting the other man a baffled look. 'What brought that on, for crying out loud? I've got no secrets from Roman.'

For a moment Sheri's smile faded a little. Goodness, the two of them were matey these days! But an amicable end to the feud notwithstanding, just why should Roman be making such an effort to help put Chris's point across to their grandfather? Was there something in it for him too? They were just two of the questions she'd like to hear answered—without any prompting from a McNamara!

'Possibly not, but *I* certainly have,' she retorted at last, her provoking smile back in place once more.

'So I've begun to realise,' put in Roman wryly at her side.

Chris gazed bewilderedly at them both and heaved a loud sigh. 'What on earth's with you two?' And to his sister, 'I thought you agreed to help with this!'

'Well, aren't I?'

'I'm starting to wonder! But couldn't you at least make an effort to be a little less antagonistic?'

'Oh, don't worry, I do ... in public,' she said explicitly, and flashed a taunting glance upwards. 'Don't I?'

'It would appear so,' conceded Roman impassively.

'You see?' Sheri's glance was sunny as it switched back to her brother.

'Do I?' he countered ruefully. 'I wish I did, but somehow I don't think I do, because for the most part you both seem to be talking in riddles to me.'

Roman laughed, a warm husky sound that had Sheri fighting to control the unexpectedly wayward feelings it aroused. 'Never mind, old son, everything's under control ... even though you may not think it,' he counselled the younger man lazily.

As long as he didn't mistakenly believe it was *his* control they were under! thought Sheri with whimsical humour as they left the room together a few minutes later.

'So where are we going to eat?' she asked jauntily as they reached the front steps of the hospital.

Roman spared her a satirical glance and turned for the car park. 'You mean you haven't already decided?'

'Was I supposed to?' She lifted innocent eyes to his and, when he acknowledged a couple of the hospital staff walking towards them, clung to his arm all the more tightly. 'You should have said.'

Halting beside a familiar green station wagon, he disengaged himself from her clasp and opened the passenger door. 'As I recall, I wasn't exactly given much of a chance to *say* anything about this meeting of ours,' he charged drily as he ushered her on to the front seat.

Sheri smothered a grin and waited until he'd taken his own seat and set the vehicle in motion. 'I was only trying to help,' she maintained in pseudo-aggrieved tones.

'Were you?' His lips twisted obliquely.

'Why else?'

By way of an answer he flicked her a sidelong glance that was drenched with mocking scepticism and, as a result, had her surmising it would be prudent to allow that particular subject to lapse.

'Well, where *are* we going for lunch?' she elected to revert to her original line of questioning instead.

'I thought the Woolsack . . . if that's acceptable to you, of course,' he added in sardonic fashion.

In retaliation, Sheri pretended to give the matter her consideration. 'Oh, I think it should be,' she finally granted in a saccharine voice. As she remembered, the Woolsack had always had the reputation of being not only the largest and classiest of the three hotels in town, but also for serving the best meals as well. It seemed the tradition hadn't altered during her absence. 'If it's not, though, we can always go somewhere else, can't we?' Her gleaming white teeth shone in a provokingly pert smile.

'Why not?' he concurred in markedly caustic accents. 'I've got nothing better to do than to drive you round all the eateries in town.'

'Oh, how considerate!' she cooed, affecting an artless pose. 'In that case, maybe we should . . .' She stopped, swallowing nervously, as a sable-fringed gaze raked over her in a manner she could only call ominous. In private, she wasn't at all certain just how far she could afford to push him. Then, with a faltering grin that she sensed was more diffident than indifferent, 'Well, perhaps not. I—er—expect you already know which is the most suitable.'

'How magnanimous of you to say so,' he aped her tongue-in-cheek demeanour sarcastically as they turned into the appropriate street and he reverse angle-parked outside the old lace-balconied hotel.

Sheri didn't comment. Even though she might have lost a little ground in that particular exchange, she was still confident of retaining the upper hand in general, and therefore could allow him such a slight victory.

With its panelled walls, ornate ceilings, elegantly carved wooden tables, and plush upholstered straight-backed chairs, the Woolsack's dining room reflected another day and age, and the fact that its décor hadn't changed a great deal over the years meant that it instantly brought to mind a host of memories for many of Goonagulla's citizens, past and present, and Sheri was no exception.

'I can often remember coming here for lunch on sale day with Dad and Grandpa and Chris during the school holidays,' she mused reminiscently after they had been shown to a table beside a tall window. 'It used to be quite a meeting place.' Her eyes scanned the almost full room with an assessing gaze and she gave a light laugh. 'It still is, by the look of it.'

'Mmm, I figured Col, at least, would prefer it if we didn't go anywhere too secluded,' Roman replied wryly, nodding a smiling acknowledgement at someone occupying another table. 'Not that I can say I was surprised, but he didn't appear to take very kindly to the idea of our dining together, and particularly not when it was thrown at him so unexpectedly.' One eyebrow quirked sardonically high. 'Don't you think a gradual approach would be more likely to succeed rather than going for broke within a couple of days?'

Sheri made an insouciant moue. 'Obviously not,'

she shrugged. 'Besides, it's the fraternisation he objects to, not the method by which he's informed of it. He took far greater exception to hearing you were to be my escort for the Ball. You see,' she smiled goadingly, 'he's of the opinion that I'm out of my mind to even *think* of having anything to do with someone with a reputation like yours where the opposite sex is concerned.'

Looking more amused than perturbed by the disclosure, he leant back in his chair, watching her with lazy-lidded eyes. 'So tell me something I couldn't work out for myself,' he invited drily. 'Like ... what else he had to say.'

'With regard to your partnering me to the Ball? W-e-ll,' she lingered over the word evocatively, warming to the subject, 'I won't bore you with all the minor details, but the gist of it was that, since I'm—er—misguided enough to agree to such a proposal, then he insists he and Grandma will also be in attendance.' Her lips curved expressively. 'Just for his own peace of mind, as it were.'

'A tactic you willingly supported, no doubt,' he surmised in an indolent drawl.

'Good heavens, no!' she denied, giving a suitably amused laugh. She considered that the best way to squash, permanently, any thoughts along the lines that she might *need* a chaperone. 'As I told Grandpa, there really wasn't likely to be any call for him to be there.' She paused, wanting to give her following trump card full emphasis. 'Which is why, of course, when he suggested it, I refused to entertain the idea of my merely meeting you at the Ball, while he drove me in to town and home again afterwards.' She cast him a not altogether unhopeful glance. 'Or would you prefer it if he did?'

'Uh-uh!' he vetoed softly, but decisively. 'That isn't

the way I operate. I prefer to collect and deliver my companions personally, thanks all the same.' He tilted his head to one side contemplatively. 'Although I note you didn't also refuse to entertain the idea of his attending the Ball.'

'No, well, I rather think he considered one victory quite sufficient. He wouldn't budge on the other,' she half laughed shakily. She was finding that lazily measuring manner of his could be quite unbalancing at times. 'Not that it really matters, does it? I mean . . .'

The arrival of a waitress to take their order brought her to an impatient halt—she was anxious to make her position clear, and to ensure Roman didn't get the wrong impression from her grandfather's insistence on being present—and in consequence she chose her meal with more haste than consideration.

'As I was saying . . .' she began again as soon as the girl left, only to be forced into holding her tongue once more owing to the wine waiter's arrival this time.

With his departure, however, Roman was the first to speak. 'Now . . . you were eager to tell me something, I believe?' he prompted—mockingly, it sounded—and she coloured selfconsciously.

'Yes, concerning Grandpa's determination to go to the Ball,' she pushed on regardless, refusing to let him disconcert her entirely. 'I was just going to say that, since we both know you're only partnering me for show, and—and solely for Chris's benefit really,' she thought it appropriate to remind him, 'then his presence shouldn't make any difference to either of us.' Her eyes held his valiantly. 'Should it?'

Roman flexed a broad shoulder. 'I wasn't planning for it to,' he admitted on a dry note.

At least that was a relief to hear, and comforted by the knowledge, Sheri began to relax again. 'Oh, I wasn't suggesting you were,' she now felt able to profess with a piquant smile. 'After all, you do have Nerissa to consider, don't you?'

'Do I?' he countered, somewhat to her surprise. Robyn couldn't possibly have got her facts mixed in that regard, could she? 'And just what do you know about Nerissa?'

'Nothing much,' she shrugged airily, and sent him a highly speculative look from beneath long silky lashes. 'Although she is your girl-friend, isn't she?' careful not to use the past tense as she had earlier when discussing the other girl's status in his life with Robyn.

'And if she is?' His brows peaked enquiringly.

'Then no doubt she'll be upset enough already by your not taking her to the Ball.' A sudden stray thought occurred. 'Unless, of course, she's to be treated differently from everyone else and you've already advised her of the reason for your—er— seeming defection.'

Roman shook his head idly. 'No, Nerissa's no wiser than anyone else,' he relayed, nodding his acceptance of the wine the waiter had returned to pour for them, and unknowingly permitting Sheri a small sigh of thankfulness on hearing his answer. If it had been otherwise, it could have had discomfiting consequences after what she'd suggested to Robyn that morning! 'All things considered, it seemed best to play it that way.'

'I see,' she nodded. And conversely, now she knew that was how he felt, she took delight in surmising, 'But won't that make her even less happy with you when she finds out afterwards?'

He gave a wry, indeterminate shrug. 'It's a distinct possibility, I guess.'

But apparently not one that worried him unduly! Sheri deduced, her lips shaping caustically. Probably because he was as assured of his own capabilities in his dealings with women as he obviously was in other spheres, her thoughts rolled on in the same tart vein. Not that it mattered to herself, of course. He could be as free and easy as he liked with his girl-friends for all she cared. In fact, as she'd observed previously, it was an attitude that suited her own purposes admirably right at the moment.

'So Nerissa is to take a back seat in order for you to assist Chris in his scheme,' she mused in ironic accents. 'That's very noble of you.'

'Hmm, I suppose that is one way of looking at it.' His lips quirked expressively.

The patent amusement in his voice rankled. 'Well, why are you going to such lengths to help him, then? Because there's something in it for you too?' she sniped.

Momentarily, Roman fixed her with a gaze of hard blue steel, and then unexpectedly he smiled, goadingly, his teeth gleaming whitely against the bronze of his skin. 'Such as?'

'How should I know?' she flared irritably, but mainly with anger at herself for having found that uneven curving of his mouth more attractive than she wanted. 'But why else would you be willing to put yourself out to such an extent?'

'Maybe, since our two families were at loggerheads for so long, purely in the cause of friendship. Did you ever think of that?' A taunting brow was lifted high.

It could be true, of course, Sheri conceded grudgingly while their meals were being served, but at the same time . . .

'And why should you want to be on friendly terms with the Taylors, instead of just speaking terms?' she still had to challenge.

'Because, fortunately, they're not all as perverse as you!'

'Oh!' Sheri glared at him indignantly, but on abruptly realising they were being covertly, though no less closely, watched by four matronly women seated at the next table, she hastily hid her resentment beneath a languishing countenance. 'You know, you really should be more careful when you say things like that,' she now chided with a winsome smile as she reached across the small table to clasp one of his hands gently with slender fingers. 'It quite spoils the effect for the onlookers when you scowl so,' she exaggerated on a purring note, 'and you really wouldn't want the most garrulous gossip in town,' one of the interested four, 'to pass the word around that our newfound—er—friendship, I think you said, appears to be striking trouble already, now would you? And after only one outing too!' She clicked her tongue in a disapproving, mocking fashion. 'Whatever might Grandpa think about our association then?'

'That would no doubt be your problem more than mine,' Roman returned indolently, although there was nothing casual in the way in which, with one swift turn of the wrist, he reversed the position of their hands so that he now very definitely had charge of hers—a move Sheri really hadn't anticipated, and, when her immediate attempt to extricate her fingers from his grip proved futile, one which had her uncomfortably feeling she had somehow lost the initiative. 'However, as for the other,' he continued with a wry, sideways glance at the next table, 'then naturally I'm also willing to do my bit for the cause—that was the way *you* put it earlier, I believe?—if that's what you want. Only too happy to oblige, in fact,' he drawled, his sable-framed eyes goading as they looked into hers, and raising her imprisoned hand he began kissing the tips of her fingers.

Gasping, Sheri felt a rush of warm blood surge into her face. This wasn't quite how she had planned it, and knowing their every action was being avidly noted did nothing to assuage either her outward embarrassment or her inner turmoil. Her fingertips suddenly seemed to have become ultra-sensitive, and the feel of his firm lips as they lightly caressed them one by one was sending unbelievable sensations racing throughout her nervous system.

'Roman!' she was finally forced into half protesting, half pleading, when it became obvious he was purposely lingering over the action, but in such a muted tone due to the proximity of the other diners that it sounded more like a sigh than a censure. 'Don't you think you're taking things a little too far? We're only supposed to be having lunch, not—not . . .'

'Mmm . . .?' he ceased momentarily in order to prompt in a lazily bantering voice.

Sheri stared at him helplessly, her thoughts refusing to come to order. Oh, God, he really did have the sexiest mouth, she found herself thinking irrelevantly, dismayingly, and immediately flushed hotly again as a result of such a treacherous lapse in her concentration. If she wasn't careful she would soon have him guessing the reason for her adolescent behaviour, she realised harassedly, and it was only the projected image of the humiliation that would engender that at last enabled her to answer him with some semblance of composure.

'I was merely going to say that I—I thought we were only supposed to be friendly . . . not f-familiar,' she said, albeit not quite as forcefully as she'd intended. 'So will you please give me back my hand,' a little flusteredly. 'I'd like to eat my lunch.'

'You think the audience has had enough for one day?' he teased, continuing to nibble at her forefinger.

Even if they hadn't, she certainly had! She was also discovering there was very little difference between him and his tormenting youngest brother either. They could each be as infuriating as the other!

'More than enough,' she retorted, and gave a thankful sigh when a sharp tug on her captive hand released it. Although only because he chose to let it go, she surmised. 'After all, we don't want to spoil them, do we?' An edge of sarcasm crept into her voice.

'Meaning, we should keep something in reserve, hmm?'

In view of the bantering overtones she thought she detected in the question, Sheri wasn't quite sure just how she should take that—as evidenced by her stammered reply. 'I—well, that remains to be seen, I suppose,' she offered lamely, and deliberately turned her attention to her meal.

The calamitous effect Roman seemed capable of having on her senses at times was something she was going to have to give some considerable thought to in order to ensure it didn't continue happening, she decided.

CHAPTER FIVE

THE following evening Sheri was dressed and ready well before the specified time Roman had arranged to call for her, and awaiting his arrival somewhat apprehensively. For although her grandfather appeared to be in a surprisingly mellow mood as he and her grandmother also readied themselves, she still wasn't too sure just what his reaction was likely to be when the younger man actually put in his appearance.

However, when the appointed time had passed and Roman still hadn't arrived, and her grandparents were about to leave themselves, she began wondering what could have been keeping him as she made periodic checks from the verandah to see if she could catch sight of any headlights in the distance that would signify his approach.

'Maybe he's changed his mind. With a reputation like his, I wouldn't put anything past him,' said her grandfather after one such fruitless check—though still without any sign of the vehemence he had displayed when he'd first learnt who her partner was to be, noted Sheri curiously. 'It's starting to look as if you'd better come with your grandmother and me, after all.'

'Oh, I don't think so, Grandpa,' she demurred wryly, guessing that was what he'd been hoping for all along. 'Why should he change his mind? He offered to partner me, I didn't ask him. In any case, he's probably just been held up somewhere, otherwise I expect he would have phoned.'

'Is that so?' Colin eyed her ironically. 'And just

what makes you so knowledgeable concerning his likely actions, eh? A few meetings at the hospital and one luncheon engagement?' he detailed disparagingly. 'No, I think you ought to come with us. That is, if you really want to be certain of getting there.'

'But he's only twenty minutes overdue!' Sheri felt bound to point out with a half laugh. 'Hardly late enough to cause a panic.'

'So who's panicking?' he retorted testily, his previous good humour suddenly deteriorating. 'I was merely suggesting . . .'

'Yes, well, I've no doubt Sheri would prefer to wait a while longer in any case,' inserted his wife with a soothing smile.

'I don't think I'll have to,' said Sheri thankfully, 'because unless I miss my guess, there's a car coming now.' The distinctive rumbling of a vehicle approaching over the hard ground was able to be heard even above their voices.

'Mmm, so there is,' agreed her grandmother with a pleased smile. 'Why don't you go out and meet him while Col brings our car around.'

Needing no second bidding, Sheri made for the door.

'You see, of course he intended coming,' Beryl's softly chiding voice sounded behind her. 'I can't understand why you thought he wouldn't.'

'Except that it hasn't been proven yet that's who it is arriving,' came Colin's dour return. 'You'll probably find it's someone else entirely.'

He sounded so positive that for a moment Sheri turned back, her forehead creasing. It was almost as if he wasn't expecting Roman to arrive, she mused perplexedly.

'Oh, and why wouldn't it be Roman?' she heard her grandmother echo her own thoughts. 'You weren't expecting anyone else to call, were you? Not when we're going out for the evening.'

'Well, perhaps it's someone who doesn't know we're planning on going out,' her husband offered, but in something of a blustering fashion to his granddaughter's ears.

Seconds later the vehicle came within range of the circle of light thrown from the verandah, enabling Sheri to inform them, 'It's not, though. That's Roman's station wagon all right.'

'You're sure?' Colin half took a step towards her, his brows drawing closely together, his tone one of— disbelief?

'W-well, yes,' she stammered in her own surprise at his incomprehensible manner. She should have been able to recognise the green vehicle, she'd been in it twice, and the last time only yesterday. 'Come and see for yourself.'

He shook his head sharply. 'No, I'll take your word for it,' he said, but in a somewhat less than pleased tone. 'Anyhow, I've got to get the car.' He promptly disappeared from the room at a stomping gait.

His action brought a rueful smile to Sheri's mobile mouth. Unfortunately, that was more like she'd expected him to behave in view of his convictions regarding Roman's social life, although it still didn't explain his previously confusing attitude. But there was little time for her to deliberate further on the matter, because her grandmother now joined her on the verandah, intent on greeting her granddaughter's escort. Even if her husband wouldn't, Beryl was certainly determined to do her utmost to make Roman feel welcome.

Sheri's own greeting was decidedly more restrained, however. When they weren't in public it was still her intention to keep a very cool distance. The more so when they were alone together, as a short time later on their way to town, with her grandfather following closely.

'You were almost half an hour late,' she therefore saw fit to rebuke as they turned out of the property and on to the highway. 'Grandpa was beginning to suggest I should go with him, after all.'

'Mmm, I bet he was.' Roman's firmly moulded lips sloped wryly.

'Meaning?'

He sent her a brief but highly sceptical glance. 'That was his intention all along, wasn't it?'

'No, of course not,' she immediately defended, despite her own similar thoughts prior to his arrival. 'How could it have been? I told you only yesterday that I'd squashed the idea.'

'So you did.' His concurrence was drily voiced. 'Unfortunately, though, it would appear Col wasn't quite of the same mind.'

'Oh, and what makes you think that?' Her eyes widened sarcastically. It merely sounded like a convenient excuse to cover his own tardiness to her.

'Just the fact that Ellimatta's gates to the back road are now—and only after offering over a hundred years of free access too—suddenly sporting brand new chains and padlocks which weren't there two days ago, that's all!' came his answer in mocking accents.

'Oh!' Sheri repeated, but this time in a rather stunned fashion, and not knowing whether to laugh at, or decry, her grandparent's hindering action. It was too much even for her to believe that it was coincidence, and especially when she herself had been the one to mention Roman's likelihood of using one of those selfsame gates in order to reach the homestead, nor when she was well aware that was exactly the area where her grandfather had said he'd been working only that morning!

'The cunning old fox!' she grinned, amusement finally winning out. 'No wonder he looked so disbelieving, not to say put out, when I said it was you arriving. He must have anticipated it taking you at least another half an hour, if not longer, to retrace your route and come via the front gate.' Her words prompted another thought and, forgetting her intention to remain aloof, she eyed the man beside her with affable curiosity. 'And that being the case, how come it didn't take you that long to reach the homestead?'

Within the vehicle's dim interior Roman's teeth shone brightly as he laughed—a vibrant sound with a perturbingly captivating effect on his listener. 'Mainly, I guess, because your grandfather isn't the only one capable of utilising a little guile when it's necessary,' he smiled with lazy attractiveness. 'I took a punt on his not having also padlocked the gate between Ellimatta and Newhaven,' the Caldwells' property, 'so I continued down the road to their gate and then cut across country from there.' He halted, his scanning gaze deepening to almost midnight blue in the darkness, and yet still not so shadowed that she couldn't distinguish the faintly taunting expression it contained. 'Luckily, my ploy proved more effective than Col's, even if it didn't enable me to arrive on time.'

Sheri looked away hastily, fiddling uncomfortably with the evening purse resting in her lap. 'Yes—well— I'm sorry Grandpa put you to so much trouble,' she felt obliged to apologise on her grandfather's behalf, even if she didn't appreciate having to do so. 'You must have found it very annoying.'

Wide shoulders lifted beneath the charcoal grey material of his impeccably tailored suit. 'Something of the kind wasn't entirely unexpected,' he surprised her by smiling wryly. 'You forget, I've known your grandfather for a long time and if I hadn't cottoned on to the way his mind works by now, then it wouldn't say much for my powers of perception.' Which were honed to razor sharpness, Sheri didn't doubt! 'Then again,' he continued, his lips slanting indolently, 'maybe I figured the end reward was worth a little aggravation, because if a mere McNamara may say so, you're looking extremely fascinating tonight, princess.'

As was he! the thought leapt unbidden into Sheri's mind, and thereby increased the hot wave of colour that was already flooding her smooth cheeks. Nor would she call him a *mere* anything, she found her thoughts running on in the same involuntary, wayward manner regardless of her attempts to bring them under control. His remark hadn't been of the nature she wanted to encourage, let alone reciprocate, even silently, and she struggled desperately to appear totally unaffected, at least outwardly, by the sudden compliment.

'Thank you,' she at last managed to acknowledge, if a little jerkily. 'You don't look too bad yourself either, if a mere Taylor may say so,' she copied with a faltering half smile, then went on quickly, 'But to return to what you were saying,' personally, she couldn't change the subject fast enough, 'you don't think Grandpa's likely to have any more—er—obstacles in store for this evening, do you?'

'Such as?'

'I wouldn't know. It never occurred to me there'd be *any*!' she grimaced.

'Then we'll just have to wait and see, I guess,' Roman smiled ruefully. 'Although really I doubt there's much more he can do this evening.' He paused, his smile widening. 'Unless, of course, he plans to let the air out of my tyres in order to ensure he at least gets to take you home again.'

'Oh, he wouldn't!' Sheri part laughed, part gasped. 'Would he?' somewhat less confidently.

'The trick isn't unknown to the Taylors ... as you should know,' came his reply in a meaningful drawl.

The prompting brought long-submerged memories racing abruptly to the fore, and Sheri grinned irrepressibly. Chris and herself had come across all three of the McNamara offspring swimming at a waterhole near their common boundary one afternoon, with the vehicle they'd used to reach the spot conveniently parked nearby. It had been a simple matter to let all the tyres down and then, because they themselves had been on horseback and safe from reprisal, stay around to gloat when their handiwork was discovered.

'But we were only kids then!' she exclaimed on a humorous note. 'Surely Grandpa wouldn't do the same today, and particularly not now that the feud's been laid to rest.' Then, without allowing him time to answer, 'In any event, as I recall, your family weren't exactly as pure as they might have been in that regard either. What about the time Chris's first car mysteriously developed four flats while he was at the sales, then?'

Roman's expression showed no remorse whatsoever. 'Poetic justice, probably,' he claimed with a laugh. 'As for Col ... well, considering how he apparently feels about my escorting his darling granddaughter, I'd say he still feels he has the right to keep his options open.'

'In what way?'

'To use whatever means happen to present themselves at the time,' she was informed in a dry tone.

'Oh,' she nodded, her own voice only slightly less ironic. 'Then I suppose we'd better keep an eye on him,' with a quick look over her shoulder towards the vehicle following behind, 'to make certain he doesn't disappear from view for any lengthy periods tonight, hadn't we?'

'It could save some unwanted bother, not to mention wasted time,' Roman conceded, his mouth tilting wryly.

The Town Hall, the customary venue for the annual Debutantes' Ball, was rapidly filling by the time they arrived. This year's décor theme was of a tropical garden and provided a perfect backdrop for the many and varied hues of the women's gowns as they thronged the high-arched foyer with their equally well-dressed escorts, awaiting friends and greeting acquaintances before making their way to their reserved tables inside.

The distinctly nervous-looking debutantes themselves, all similarly clad in traditional white, together with their just as young and edgy dinner-suited partners, could be seen in an ante-room to one side of the entrance where they were doubtless receiving last-minute instructions and reminders from the ladies who had planned and co-ordinated the occasion on their behalf.

Inside the hall long damask-covered tables supported huge vases of orchids, hibiscus, and frangipani, the latter permeating the air with a perfume redolent of warm summer nights and white coral beaches. Along the walls stood tubs and pots filled with palms, and vines, and umbrella trees, while here and there bushy crotons displayed an incredible array of leaf shape and brilliant colour. The official dais had been decorated solely in red and white, someone having somehow managed to procure a giant out-of-season waratah, the

State's impressive floral emblem, to take pride of place.

Gradually the crowd began to disperse a little as some moved inside to their tables, Roman and Sheri deciding to do likewise. However, as they walked towards the main doors Sheri caught the sound of her grandfather's gruff voice behind them and, without halting her strolling pace, half turned to discover both him and her grandmother only a foot or so away.

'Grandpa, you should be ashamed of yourself,' she reproached in a soft voice so that only they could hear, her expression one of amused annoyance. 'How could you do such a thing? Particularly after letting me think you'd accepted the idea!'

In spite of the sheepish look that came over his face, Colin obviously wasn't about to admit anything as he countered, 'Do what?' with innocently raised brows.

'Yes, do what, dear?' echoed her grandmother in puzzlement.

'Put padlocks on both gates to the back road so Roman would have to go the long way round.'

Beryl immediately cast her husband a narrowing glance. 'Did you do that?' she demanded to know.

He half shrugged awkwardly. 'I—well, I didn't want a repeat of what happened to Chris with just anyone able to get on to the property,' he excused his actions in testy tones. 'Anyway, it didn't seem to slow him down much.' The corners of his mouth pulled inwards in a disgruntled grimace.

'Only because he had the foresight to cut through Newhaven instead,' Sheri inserted.

'Oh!' her grandfather grunted in patent disappointment—the vexation being due to his own lack of foresight in failing to prevent access from there too, Sheri suspected ruefully. 'Well, it doesn't matter now, does it? You travelled in with him, after all.'

'No thanks to you, apparently,' his wife reproved wryly. And to Sheri, 'But don't you worry, dear. I'll see nothing else happens to mar your evening, believe me.'

Colin looked down at her askance. 'For heaven's sake!' he expostulated, albeit with something of a splutter. 'Anyone would think it was a crime for a man to want to protect his own property.'

'Mmm, but that all depends on just who you're trying to protect from whom, and for what reason, dear,' Beryl replied smoothly and, as all four of them passed through the doorway, she gave her granddaughter a reassuring smile before guiding her husband towards their allotted table.

'What was all that about?' asked Roman as Sheri turned to the front again.

'I was having words with Grandpa about the reason for those locks,' she laughed.

'And . . .?' The corners of his mouth turned up lazily.

Finding her senses responding with a disturbing attraction, Sheri dragged her eyes away swiftly. 'He reckoned they were to prevent a repeat of what befell Chris, although it was clear that wasn't the reason at all. Even Grandma didn't think so,' she relayed in as even a voice as possible. 'Although there is some good news.' Her green eyes lit with humour. 'Grandma also said she would ensure that nothing else of a like nature happened this evening.'

'Now that does sound promising,' he agreed. 'Do I detect an ally thereabouts?' His head inclined enquiringly.

'I—I guess so,' she owned reluctantly, shrugging. 'At least she didn't object like Grandpa did when she heard I was going out with you.' She sent him a mocking look from the cover of thick, curling lashes.

'Grandma would give anyone a chance to prove themselves, no matter what their reputation.'

Roman grinned impenitently, a finger beneath her chin tipping her face up to his unexpectedly. 'And how about you . . . eh?'

'M-me too, I suppose,' she abruptly found herself granting involuntarily on a husky note as his touch sent shivers of awareness racing down her spine.

Roman looped an arm about her shoulders, a heart-stopping smile moulding his shapely mouth as he gazed down at her. 'That's a relief to know,' he said softly. 'Because there's been a couple of times when I've wondered just exactly whose side you *were* on!'

Sheri pulled herself together with an effort, and managed to unobtrusively slip from under his arm as they rounded a table. Whatever was the matter with her allowing a purely physical attraction to affect her so?

'I'm on Chris's side, of course,' she said implicitly, accompanied by what she trusted was a satisfactorily surprised laugh. She didn't want him thinking it was him, personally, she was supporting. And just for good measure, 'I would have thought I'd already proved that by suggesting, in front of Grandpa too, that we met for lunch yesterday.'

'Except that I couldn't quite decide whether that was actually for his benefit . . . or some other more obscure reason.' His lips twisted wryly.

Swallowing hard, she executed a passably artless shrug. 'What other reason could there be?'

'That's what had me wondering,' he drawled in an extremely dry tone.

'Oh, well, don't let it spoil your evening thinking about it,' she recommended, not altogether facetiously. The last thing she wanted was for him to deliberate on the matter. He just might come up with the correct answer! 'There's Laurel and her family over there. Shall we join them?'

Of necessity their table was a large one, catering as it did for not only Laurel's family but their cousins, the McNamaras, as well, many of whom Sheri hadn't become reacquainted with since her return until now. So by the time all the customary acknowledgements had been dispensed with and they were all seated, most of the other tables were also filled, the band was in place, and the official party containing the Government Senator to whom the debutantes were to be presented was just about ready to make its entrance.

In the short space before it appeared, Sheri used the opportunity to more thoroughly survey not only the occupants of her own table, but others elsewhere in the hall too. Opposite her, Morgan, the second eldest from the branch of the McNamara family she knew best, was talking desultorily with his attractive wife. A marriage as Sheri already knew, via Chris, that had taken place some three or four years ago, shortly after his parents had retired to the coast and he had purchased a property of his own.

Perhaps not surprisingly, though, it was on Hayden, the youngest, that her gaze remained longest. Naturally enough, since he was only a year or two older than herself, he had altered physically far more than his two brothers, and in truth she found it a little difficult initially to reconcile the strapping young man beside Robyn with the image she had of him from childhood. At least that was until he'd happened to grin a quick-fire response to something Roman said, and then she'd had no trouble whatsoever in doing so, for although he might have grown into an unexpectedly engaging specimen of manhood, after that sudden roguish curving of his wide mouth she'd had no doubts at all that on occasion he could still be as teasing as ever.

With her glance moving idly on, Sheri came to the conclusion that she knew no one at the next table and passed on to the one alongside it. Here, she discovered quite a number of familiar faces, but as she allowed her gaze to travel slowly over its occupants she suddenly, dismayingly, found her eyes colliding with another pair of so dark a brown as to appear black, and which were staring with dagger-like intensity directly back at her! Oh, hell—Nerissa! she gulped, instantly recognising the alabaster-pale, but perfectly sculpted features framed within remembered masses of almost blue-black hair, but rather than look away immediately as she felt like doing, made herself return the older girl's rancorous stare defiantly for a few moments before pretending to resume her casual interest in her surroundings.

And pretend was certainly right! she was forced to concede wryly a few short seconds later on realising that not another face had registered. It seemed her thoughts were already too occupied to allow any other information to intrude. Unaccountably, the most recurring one concerning the man beside her. Had Roman known Nerissa would be here tonight, even if not as his partner? she wondered, watching him surreptitiously from the corner of her eye. Or was he so confident of his ability to soothe her ruffled feelings at a later date that it was of little concern to him if she'd come or not? A touch of sarcasm found its way into her musings. Probably the latter, she decided with a grimace, and promptly determined to do all in her power to make any explaining he had to do as difficult as possible!

To everyone's delight, and relief, the presentations went off without a hitch. The dozen or so girls making their deep curtsies with only an occasional sign of a wobble; their teenage escorts carrying out their duties, if not with aplomb, then at least with creditable endeavour; and during the Debutante Waltz that followed, gallantly managed to appear as if it wasn't the first time in their lives for the majority of them that they'd danced so formally.

Then, once the official part of the evening was completed, it was time for everyone to relax as drinks were ordered and dinners served, and the dance floor became well patronised.

'Shall we?' Roman turned to ask Sheri, indicating the dancing. His head lowered disconcertingly close, his eyes teasing. 'It'll make good propaganda.'

'Then you give me no choice. By all means let's adjourn to the dance floor,' she quipped with appropriate lightness after only a slight hesitation. After all, this was how she'd always intended to play it, wasn't it? With her monopolising every possible moment of his time until he pleaded for relief from her presence? 'I see Grandpa is already watching us,' she went on to remark ruefully on noting her grandparent's eyes following their progress as they headed for a space within the crowd of dancing couples. That she had also noticed other eyes—hostile, smouldering eyes—watching them, she didn't see fit to divulge. If he didn't already know, *that* he could discover all for himself! she resolved with unadulterated relish.

Roman immediately swept her close within his arms and began moving in time to the beat of the music. 'Then we'd best make it worth his while, hadn't we?' he drawled.

Sheri could only nod weakly, once again caught unawares. The way she had imagined it, she was the one who was supposed to give the appearance of chasing after him by moving provocatively closer. Not him depriving her of the initiative yet again, just as he'd done the day before! And definitely she wasn't supposed to be so ungovernably conscious of his muscled length as it pressed against her slender form that she was hardly aware of what she was doing! If she didn't take hold of herself soon she could very well find the advantage was all his, and in view of the way she was reacting right at present that was something she didn't dare contemplate. A thought so alarming that it temporarily drove all others out of her mind and, as a result, proved to be just the incentive she needed to enable her to press on with her own plan for putting him on the defensive instead.

With a deep and, she hoped, steadying breath, she slid her left hand across his shoulder to lightly caress the nape of his neck before twining a curl of dark hair around her forefinger experimentally. 'Why does it always seem to be men who have the lovely curly hair?' she tilted her face upwards to smile ingenuously. His was a mass of thick, loosely waving curls she would have welcomed possessing.

For his part, Roman returned her gaze with marked scepticism. 'Just what are you playing at, sweetheart?' he chose to quiz ironically rather than answer her spurious question.

Sheri hunched one golden-skinned shoulder innocently even as she hid a pleased smile at the dubious note in his voice. 'What makes you think I'm playing at anything?' If he did but know it, she was really quite serious, both about his hair and what she was doing. 'Because I said you had nice hair? But it is,' she insisted, and as if to emphasise her point deliberately continued winding her fingers within the curls at the back of his head. 'Or hasn't anyone ever complimented you on it before?' She cast him a bantering sidelong glance.

The arm encircling her slim form tightened a little. 'Not that I can recall,' he revealed drily. 'And definitely not in the middle of a dance floor.'

'Well, they do say there's a first time for everything, don't they?' she propounded in playful fashion.

'Mmm ... so they do,' he concurred on such a subtle note that her smile slipped a little and she unconsciously began gnawing at her underlip. Had he meant to imply something by that? she speculated warily. An apprehensiveness which apparently wasn't lost on Roman, because he promptly broke in on her thoughts with a facetious-sounding, 'Anything wrong?'

Suddenly realising what she was doing, Sheri forced the corners of her mouth upwards again. 'N-no, how could there be?' she countered as unconcernedly as she was able. Then, chancing on something she hoped would distract him, 'I mean, you said yourself we should make Grandpa's watching us worthwhile, and he must be getting the message by now, surely.'

'Oh, undoubtedly,' he was willing to concede, but with something of a sardonic nuance in his tone that did little to assist her to regain her equanimity. 'Though just what particular message that might be could be something else again, of course.' The satirical edge to his voice was quite pronounced now and had Sheri resuming chewing at her bottom lip.

'I don't know what you mean,' she claimed cautiously. She wasn't too certain she even wanted to know!

'No?' A well-shaped brow rose expressively. 'You mean, you haven't been promoting the idea that Nerissa is now something of the past as far as I'm concerned ... owing to *your* having replaced her?'

Oh, lord, Robyn must have been doing some

talking! And judging by his expression it would be doubtful if any denials would be believed. 'I—well, you didn't appear too worried about her during lunch yesterday,' she stammered accusingly instead.

'Except that as I hear it, you'd conveniently disposed of her as—er—competition, *prior* to that meeting,' Roman relayed succinctly.

It was difficult to tell whether he was annoyed or not, but then it had never been her intention to make things easy for him. 'It seemed reasonable to do so at the time . . . to help convince Grandpa when word got around, you understand,' she smiled pertly.

'Ah, yes,' he nodded. 'Just another bit for the cause, eh?'

Her smile widened provokingly. 'I couldn't have put it better myself.'

To her surprise that brought a resonant laugh issuing from his strong, tanned throat. 'Okay, sweetheart, if that's the way it's to be, it would seem I've acquired a new girl-friend for myself, wouldn't it?' he drawled, then bent his head so that his lips were only a disturbing hair's breadth from her ear, to add somewhat mockingly, 'One from whom I'm sure I shall rapidly become inseparable.'

Sheri jerked her head away rapidly, her emerald eyes clouding with something akin to dismay. Somewhere, somehow, she must have said or done something radically wrong, she groaned inwardly. That they become inseparable had been the basis of *her* plan to rile *him*! He wasn't supposed to equably accept the idea, and he very definitely wasn't supposed to have suggested the same himself! That had defeated the very reason she had devised the scheme in the first place, and now she was being put in the position of having to cast about frantically for an excuse to thwart the suddenly not so attractive idea. Happily, though, she abruptly hit upon what she thought could be the very thing.

'I doubt even Grandma would be in favour of that,' she said in a rush.

'Oh, and why not?' Roman's eyes watched her lazily. 'You said yourself she had no objection to you accompanying me this evening.'

'Yes, but that's just it, you see. One or two supposed dates she would find totally acceptable, but if there were too many she may feel obliged to mention it to Mother ... and Mother would categorically disapprove,' she concluded with a half smile of feigned regret.

'And you, of course, always do as your mother instructs,' he taunted.

He was back to suggesting she didn't make her own decisions again, Sheri fumed, diverted, and it still nettled. 'No, I do not!' she flared automatically. 'But ...'

'Then that disposes of that objection ... *if* and when it should occur,' Roman cut in, expressively wry, and had her flashing him a fulminating glance.

'You didn't let me finish,' she charged on a acid note, then had to stop in order to return the greeting of another couple passing by.

'Mmm ...?' Roman prompted immediately the other pair had disappeared again into the crowd surrounding them, but with such a goading inflection that Sheri could have slapped him.

Instead, she gritted her teeth, and gave him back a look as chafing as his own. 'I was going to say ... but apart from anything else, *I* do still have Todd to consider,' she disclosed with pointed emphasis.

If she'd thought to confuse him with the use of the unfamiliar name then Roman was only too ready to show her how mistaken she was by smoothly asserting,

'I don't know why. According to my information he's about due to be dropped, anyway, isn't he?'

Sheri could hardly believe her ears. So Robyn wasn't the only one who'd been doing some talking. It appeared Chris hadn't exactly been backward in that department either! And right at the moment she could quite cheerfully have slapped him as well for having discussed her at all with his neighbour.

'That's as may be!' was the most she was prepared to concede, stormily. 'But *if* I should decide to do so, I'll be the one to tell him. I don't want to give Mother the opportunity of saying something to him about us.'

'An extremely unlikely circumstance, wouldn't you say?' Up went those all too explicit brows once more.

'I don't see why,' it was her turn to contend now.

'Because as I was also given to understand . . . it's your mother who's most in favour of the alliance, and that being the case . . .' he smiled aggravatingly, 'then I very much doubt she would willingly say or do anything that might conceivably give him reason to believe he didn't hold—er—pride of place in your life any more.'

His assumption was too damned accurate for her to even bother trying to dispute it—thanks once again to Chris! she seethed impotently. 'That still doesn't mean Mother will like the idea if she comes to hear of it,' she was reduced to protesting in a distinctly weaker manner.

'But as you're so adamant she doesn't make your decisions for you, then that really shouldn't present any problems, should it?' He paused, his eyes filling with lazy provocation. 'I mean, as you were so disposed to point out, it is all in aid of convincing Col . . . on Chris's behalf. So for tomorrow, I'll pick you up around ten, shall I?' He took her acquiescence for granted.

'I—I . . .' He was moving too fast for her and, to her despair, it showed. 'In order to do what?' she at last managed to query, but in something of a croak.

'Does it matter particularly?'

'I suppose not,' she grimaced fatalistically, since she seemed to have exhausted all the objections she could think of on the spur of the moment. Then, as a more spirited and definitely more pungent afterthought, 'All depending on just what you've got in mind, of course!'

'Oh?' The mocking look that came over his face had her wishing she'd held her tongue instead of thoughtlessly giving rise to the very speculation she'd previously been at such pains to prevent happening. 'And just what do you imagine I might have in mind?'

'How should I know?' she attempted to rectify her mistake by shrugging as insouciantly as possible. 'I've never really even been on speaking terms, let alone social ones, with a McNamara before.'

Roman's lips sloped crookedly. 'Then it will be a first for both of us, won't it?'

She hadn't thought of it like that. 'I guess so,' she was only too willing to agree, however, in her relief that he appeared to have taken her excuse at face value. Nonetheless, she was even more grateful when the music finally ceased and they returned to their seats. All of a sudden she was finding Roman too perturbing, in too many ways, to remain in his sole company any longer than was absolutely necessary.

Sheri's next dance was with Hayden, her childhood tormentor. Only these days, as he very soon discovered, she was more than able to give as good as she got in the teasing stakes—a fact that appeared to entertain rather than irritate him—and although she rapidly, ruefully, came to the conclusion that his continued use of the nickname he had always labelled her with, Red, wasn't purely done to annoy any more, but was seemingly as automatic as breathing on his part and a habit it was doubtful would ever be broken, she did find to her astonishment that he had grown into rather a personable member of the opposite sex with whom she could converse quite readily.

Meanwhile, as they passed their table she also became aware that Roman's seat was vacant, whereupon some impulse had her eyes promptly flashing to where Nerissa had been sitting, and her soft lips shaping into a derisive grimace on finding her intuition correct and him to be leaning casually over the back of the other girl's chair as he responded to her obvious blandishments with every evidence of smiling enjoyment.

More fool Nerissa to be taken in by someone so superficial! she scorned disdainfully, her head unconsciously angling defiantly higher, and for the rest of the evening set about showing Roman—in particular, for some unknown reason—that it was of supreme indifference to her whether he returned to his own table or not because she was just as capable of enjoying herself without his presence. Probably more, if the truth were known!

A circumstance that obviously hadn't escaped her grandfather's notice either, she realised when he came to claim her for a dance, for as soon as they began moving to the music he remarked bluntly, 'Well, you certainly seem to be the life and soul of the party. I just hope, for your sake, that it doesn't rebound on you later.'

Sheri hunched one shoulder, lightly dismissive. 'I can't think why it should. I'm only having a good time.'

'Due to Roman being your partner?'

'Amongst other things,' she avoided answering directly, remembering her brother's hopes.

'Hmm!' was his patently discontented response which had her sensing a diversion might be politic. There was no point in pushing something he was still so clearly opposed to. With someone as singleminded as he was, that could quite possibly bring about the completely opposite effect to the one desired.

'So how are you and Grandma enjoying yourselves, then?' she asked instead.

'Oh, all right, I suppose,' he allowed offhandedly. Dancing had never been known to be exactly one of his favourite pastimes. 'Your grandmother's certainly in her element, though, catching up on all the news she's missed from around town.' He halted momentarily, eyeing her with a lowering gaze. 'Especially the little morsel concerning her granddaughter having her hand kissed in the Woolsack's dining room yesterday!'

So that had made its way back to him already, had it? 'Actually, it wasn't my hand, it was my fingers,' Sheri corrected with assumed nonchalance. The memory of the discomposing effect the action had had on her at the time abruptly returning in full force, destroying any chance she might have had of discussing it with any degree of impassivity.

Her grandfather snorted disapprovingly. 'Well, he'd better not try anything similar when I'm around or there'll be trouble, I can tell you!'

'Oh, Grandpa, there was no harm done,' she couldn't help smiling wryly at his attitude. At least, no permanent harm, she amended reassuringly for her own benefit. 'Besides . . .'

'You liked it, I suppose?' he interposed on an ironically growled note.

Well . . .' She made her smile soften evocatively, surmising it was time to do a little more for the cause again. 'As I've said before, I like *him*.' Which may have been a convenient way of evading the issue, but which also, she unexpectedly realised to her consternation, might have been closer to the truth than she wished it to be.

'Huh!' grunted Colin significantly, her reply apparently bringing him no joy either, and for a time lapsed into a silence Sheri accepted gratefully. For the present she had more than enough disturbing thoughts of her own to analyse without seeking to debate his.

Thoughts she still hadn't managed to explain away entirely to her satisfaction by the time their dance came to an end, however, and rather than return to the table with them in such a strangely unsettled state, she made for the powder room instead in the hope that the extra time so afforded would provide her with the opportunity to regain at least some measure of the equanimity she desired before resuming her place.

There were only two others using the room when Sheri arrived, neither of whom she knew particularly well, but no sooner had they departed than the door almost immediately swung open again to admit someone else. Someone she knew only too well this time as on turning her head absently to see who it might be she came face to face with Nerissa. Any notion of carefully arranging her thoughts now fled from Sheri's mind altogether and she watched the dark-haired girl's sauntering approach warily. She didn't believe for one minute that mere coincidence had brought them both there at precisely the same time.

'I heard you were back,' Nerissa began with a sneer, perching on the arm of one of the two deep chairs the carpeted room possessed, and extracting a cigarette from her gold-linked evening bag. 'So how long are you planning on honouring us with your presence after all these years?'

Sheri smoothed a few loosened hairs into place with the aid of the wall-length mirror. 'I haven't decided yet,' she shrugged. Then, in return for the other girl's gibing tone, she couldn't refrain from adding, 'It may even be for good.'

Behind her, Nerissa sucked in a sharp breath. 'Because of Roman?' she grated.

Now they were getting closer to the heart of the matter! 'Could be,' Sheri wasn't above alleging with a smile.

Nerissa drew on her cigarette furiously. 'You'll never hold him, you know,' she smirked, but on a brittle note.

'So says the voice of experience, hmm?'

Momentarily, the older girl's ruby glossed lips thinned, her dark eyes glittering fiercely, then she gave a lightly amused laugh. 'Hardly, when I only had to lift a finger this evening to have him running back to my side,' she scoffed.

It wasn't a claim she could dispute, Sheri realised disappointedly, a peculiar sinking feeling abruptly making itself felt in the pit of her stomach. 'Not for long, though,' she still had to remind. Indeed, she'd been somewhat surprised herself at the brief time Roman had actually spent with his usual partner.

'Well, naturally!' Nerissa laughed again, condescendingly. 'We didn't want to embarrass you too much by making it obvious to everyone that we would rather have been together.'

'Oh?' The contention brought a sardonic gleam to Sheri's green eyes. She had certainly never known Nerissa to be concerned about anyone's finer feelings before—just the opposite, usually!—and with herself the subject of any likely embarrassment she didn't doubt that would have been the object tonight too, if at all possible. The knowledge gave her the confidence to quiz wryly, 'Then if that was the case, I wonder why he invited me to the Ball and not you.'

'He was probably just using you to get back at me because we'd had a little tiff,' Nerissa simpered.

'A ploy that would appear to have been most successful, then.' Sheri's lips twitched humorously.

Nerissa expelled a stream of smoke towards the ceiling. 'What could possibly make you think that?'

'For a start, the distinctly hostile glare you greeted me with when our glances first met earlier this evening; and secondly, the fact that you apparently felt the need to warn me off with the clearly discouraging claim that I wouldn't be able to hold Roman's attention,' Sheri had no reservations about informing her drily.

'Only because it was in your best interests!'

'And not your own, of course!' The amused cast to Sheri's mouth became even more noticeable.

Seeing it, Nerissa rose to her feet swiftly, her pale cheeks stained with chagrined colour. 'Don't you dare laugh at me!' she blazed irately as she stalked across the room. 'Granted, he may be paying you some little attention now, but only, I expect, to ensure your grandfather doesn't begin that infantile feud again, and certainly it won't be for very long. You can take my word for it, *I'll* see to that!' stabbing her cigarette emphatically in the younger girl's direction as she returned to her confidently taunting manner.

Only by stepping back quickly did Sheri avoid having her dress burnt—as she suspected had been intended—and as a result her own gaze turned scornful. 'How? By throwing yourself at him as you were doing a little while ago?' she mocked.

'You should talk! You weren't exactly playing hard to get either while on the dance floor, were you? Winding your fingers in his hair!' Nerissa jeered derisively, wrathfully.

Oh, she had seen that, had she? 'Mmm, but then neither was he objecting, was he?'

A fact Nerissa would obviously have preferred not to have pointed out to her, if her seething expression was any indication. 'No doubt only because he didn't wish to draw even more humiliating attention to yourselves by doing so in public!' Her upper lip curled contemptuously. 'Not that he should have worried, of course, because with someone who likes to make an exhibition of themselves to the extent you obviously do, I shouldn't imagine you even know how to feel abashed!' She dropped her cigarette to the floor and coolly ground it into the carpet.

The arrogantly destructive act had Sheri eyeing her with open distaste. 'Well, I certainly try not to when you're around!' she retorted. 'I learnt that lesson a long time ago when your idea of fun was to hold all of us younger children up to ridicule in front of your equally insensitive clique of friends.'

Nerissa's eyes shone with a venomous glint. 'Then it's a pity you didn't also learn to keep your grasping hands off someone else's property, because I'm telling you here and now that Roman is mine! *Mine*, do you hear?' she stressed on a vehement note.

She was welcome to him! grimaced Sheri, although that was a revelation she meant to keep entirely to herself. 'But only if *I* feel inclined to give him back to you, of course,' she goaded.

'You bitch!' A furious hand was swung towards Sheri's face but which, since she had half anticipated something of the kind—it wasn't the first time she had seen the dark-haired girl in action—she was able to sidestep easily. 'You'll pay for that, you see if you don't!' Nerissa threatened malevolently. 'You always were a brazen slut who needed to be put in your place!'

'While *you* were always a malicious hag just about everyone loathed intensely!' Sheri had no compunction in retaliating in kind, and turned for the exit. It hadn't been a meeting of her choosing, and a little of Nerissa went a very long way!

For a few seconds, though, it seemed as if the other girl meant to react physically again as she took a step forward with a hand already partly raised, but to Sheri's relief the door swung inwards at that moment to admit Robyn and Nerissa had to be content with a savage glare as she passed them both before storming out into the hall.

'Wow! What was that for?' quizzed Robyn with an expressive half laugh. Then, without allowing time for a reply, she went on, 'You'd been gone for so long that I came to see if anything was wrong.'

Sheri's lips curved ruefully. 'Yes, well, Nerissa and I were having a little talk.'

'I can't guess what about.' A wry smile caught at her friend's own mouth.

'No, I just bet you can't,' returned Sheri with feeling, and nodded towards the door. 'So shall we return to the table?'

'Without any explanations?' in patent disappointment.

'Without any explanations,' repeated Sheri humorously, although nonetheless decisively. Tonight, Roman really wasn't a subject she even wanted to think about, let alone discuss.

CHAPTER SIX

EVENTUALLY the Ball came to a finish in the early hours of the morning with everyone agreeing that it had been a resounding success as they made their leisurely farewells and headed for the car park. Along with the rest, Sheri and Roman did likewise, her grandparents lost to sight for a time.

'Well, at least we still have four inflated tyres,' Roman announced with a smile after a swift check of the station wagon. And as he saw her into the passenger seat, 'Although I'm surprised Col isn't breathing down my neck at this point. I quite expected to have him tailing me even closer on the way home than he did getting here.'

'Don't worry, I've no doubt he will,' Sheri asserted drily as he took his seat beside her. The more so, probably, since learning of that episode at the Woolsack!

Sure enough, before they could complete reversing out of the parking area, the two older Taylors made their appearance; Colin hurrying his wife along as quickly as she was able, and Beryl obviously protesting volubly about his haste.

Inside the station wagon, Sheri swiftly started a conversation in the hope of diverting Roman's attention from the vehicle now rapidly closing the gap behind them. If her grandfather wasn't careful he would be giving the younger man the very ideas she had done her best to suppress and which, if he did but realise it, he most definitely would prefer not to see raised!

Fortunately, the subject she chanced upon, cotton—it seemed appropriate in view of her promise to help her brother's cause with their grandfather—was one which enabled her to question her companion at length, but if he guessed there was a secondary reason prompting her to do so he didn't show it, and by the time they had to stop to open the first of Ellimatta's gates, she doubted there was very much that hadn't been explained to her regarding the crop.

As was normal, they left the gate for the last car through to close, and continued on to the next one. There were three altogether before they finally reached the homestead where the verandah light was the only one visible in the otherwise pitch black surroundings. Swinging the car around, Roman brought it to a halt a short distance from the house just outside the circle of light and sat for a moment with his hands resting on the wheel as he looked towards the headlights still approaching along the track. The last two gates had required lifting rather than swinging open, and because of his greater agility and strength the space between the two vehicles had increased considerably since reaching the property.

Slowly, a wry grin began to ease across his firm lips, sending Sheri's pulse rocketing as he half turned in his seat to trace the exposed line of her jaw with the tip of his forefinger. 'Col sure doesn't intend us to have any time alone together if he can help it, does he?' he drawled, and indicating with a slight nod of his head the now fast nearing headlights.

Sheri swallowed nervously and forced her eyes to the front, wishing her grandfather had already arrived. 'Why should we need any time alone together, anyway?' she countered shakily.

'Mainly because you seem to have been doing your

damnedest to ensure he expects us to, I guess,' he elucidated in a mocking tone.

'O-only in public, though,' she attempted to qualify aloofly. 'But just because he suspects your intentions . . .' A hand suddenly ensnaring her chin had her breaking off with a startled gasp.

'Then maybe, for once, I should give him a reason for his suspicions,' Roman threatened. 'While making another worthwhile contribution to the cause at the same time, of course,' he added tauntingly as his mouth descended inexorably on to hers.

Sheri made a small, outraged sound deep in her throat and began pushing against his broad chest furiously. This was exactly what she had wanted to avoid and now, for an even more imperative reason, she knew why! He was drawing a response from her waywardly parting lips even as she fought to escape!

It was an intolerable situation, but one from which it seemed he wasn't prepared to release her, and as the sinewed bands of his arms curved round her, effectually trapping her hands between them while strong fingers destroyed her upswept hairstyle as they threaded between the russet-coloured strands, she felt herself succumbing helplessly to the sensuous exhilaration of his demanding mouth, just as she had once before.

It was the rumble of advancing wheels that brought her back to the realisation of what she was doing, and gave her the strength to renew her attempts to be free and to twist her head away from the mind-drugging contact.

'Grandpa will kill you for this!' she heaved jerkily.

'I doubt it,' Roman demurred in a warm, husky voice that had her heartbeat accelerating ungovernably again, and making no move to loosen his hold on her. 'Not while your grandmother's present, anyway, and especially not when he sees you aren't struggling.'

'*I am struggling!*' she protested hotly, trying desperately, but futilely, to extricate herself once more.

A mocking light flashed in the depths of his blue eyes. 'Now!' he drawled expressively.

Sheri crimsoned. It was humiliating enough knowing in her own mind that he'd been able to overcome her defences with such consummate ease, but for him to remark on it made it doubly mortifying.

'And so I was before,' she maintained, but on something of a choking note that did little to make it sound convincing. 'As you very well know.' Her emerald green eyes connected briefly, resentfully, with his.

Removing one arm from about her—the other was more than adequate to ensure she couldn't stray—Roman tilted her face upwards, his lips only unsettling inches above her own. 'Then I might suggest you don't do so any more,' he murmured ironically, his breath soft and vaguely intoxicating against her flushed skin. 'Otherwise you could just find all your previously provocative little efforts have gone for nought.'

Did he mean with regard to her grandfather, or . . . himself? Oh, God, he couldn't possibly think all those purposely flirtatious actions had been solely in order to encourage *this*, could he? She shrank from the idea in horror even as his shapely mouth claimed hers yet again, and then she had more immediate problems to contend with.

Admittedly, she attempted to squirm free of his grasp, but to her increased consternation the movement only served to emphasise the closeness of his rugged form as it encountered the softness of hers, and aroused the same heated awareness of his heady masculinity that had so disturbingly assailed her at the

Ball. Through the flimsy material of her gown she could feel the ridged muscles of his thigh hard alongside hers, the wide expanse of his chest pressing against the rounded curves of her swelling breasts bringing involuntarily hardening nipples to a wanton prominence, and with a muted sob of defeat her already weakening exertions finally ceased altogether.

Seconds later her grandfather's vehicle swept past them, but as Roman had predicted, it didn't even slow, let alone stop, but continued on around to the garage. Its passing left only the fitful light from the verandah to alleviate the total darkness once more, and Sheri to resolve that if no assistance was to be forthcoming from that direction, then she at least would valiantly endeavour to see Roman wasn't afforded a second opportunity to taunt her with her unbidden response. It was the only way left to her if she was to salvage any of her pride at all!

Roman, meanwhile, appeared to have other ideas, because although he relinquished her lips shortly after her grandfather had passed, it soon became evident he hadn't done so as a prelude to releasing her entirely, but merely so that he could continue his devastating assault on her unbelievably heightened senses in other ways. But ways, as Sheri swiftly came to realise, she was as helpless to overcome as she had the other—no matter how rigidly she attempted to hold herself.

The feel of his lips as they leisurely explored the honey-gold skin of her neck and bared shoulder was sending electrifying impulses to the very extremities of her body, and kindling sensuous desires of her own she had never before experienced. The touch of his hand did the same, igniting fires of passion as it wandered unhindered from the flaring curve of her hip to the fullness of a throbbing breast, until it became impossible to deny any longer the demands making themselves felt so potently within her, and she melted against him pliantly in ultimate surrender.

With a stifled groan, Roman returned his attention to her mouth, feeling it open willingly to his lips now, his own caresses immediately becoming more persuasive than dominant as a result, and at last allowing her to slide her hands free. As soon as they were, Sheri promptly proceeded to wind them ardently about his neck, her fingers burying themselves amid the dark curls covering the back of his head, her breathing deepening convulsively when a tanned hand probed the diagonal neckline of her gown to cup a taut breast. She didn't know what mechanism he had triggered inside her, but she seemed powerless to suppress the quickening emotions that were filling her with a warm ache of nameless longing. Emotions, unaccountably only he had ever evoked.

Then suddenly Roman was raising his head, his attractively sculptured mouth quirking crookedly as he gazed down into her flushed and drowsy-eyed features. 'Somehow I think we'd better call it a day, princess. While we're still able.' He rubbed ruefully at his jaw.

Sheri swallowed hard as full comprehension of just how uninhibitedly she had responded to his love-making hit home, and averted her face hastily as embarrassment swamped her. 'Yes, of course,' she acceded stiffly, trying to restore some order to her rumpled hair with unsteady fingers. She knew she should have felt relieved that he'd stopped when he did—how could she have let it go so far?—but all she seemed to be experiencing was a humiliating sense of rejection. 'It's getting late and Grandma might be waiting up for me. She's always liked to make sure everyone was in before she went to bed.' Aware she was beginning to babble, she fumbled with the door catch, anxious only to escape. 'But thank you for escorting me to the Ball. I had a very enjoyable time.'

'Sheri . . . *for God's sake!*' Before she could set a foot outside the opening door Roman caught hold of her arm and swung her back to face him again. 'I didn't suggest you leave because I *wanted* you to go!' he exclaimed forcefully. He brushed his knuckles across her soft cheek as he continued in a gentler tone, 'I thought it was in your best interests, that's all.'

In other words, to save her from her own lack of control! she supposed bitterly. He, presumably, having proved all he wanted by subduing her resistance so effortlessly!

'And when I need a McNamara to tell me what's in my best interests, it will be a sorry day!' she flared defensively, all her old feuding instincts racing to the fore.

For a moment Roman's blue eyes blazed fiercely and his grip on her arm tightened to a painful degree, followed by an almost contemptuous gesture whereby he withdrew his hand completely. 'Then I suggest you make tracks before this becomes an even sorrier one!' he bit out significantly.

His meaning was plain and Sheri had no wish to tempt fate twice in such a short space of time. 'If you remember, that's exactly what I was trying to do . . . before *you* stopped me,' she sniped over one shoulder as she scrambled out of the station wagon swiftly and slammed the door behind her.

'Mmm, I should have known better, shouldn't I? It always was impossible to talk sense to a contrary Taylor!' he gibed right back.

'Oh?' she seethed, glaring at him through the open window. 'Does Chris know that's how you feel?'

'Fortunately, your brother appears to have been made in a different mould. He *knows* his own mind!'

'Knows it? Or naïvely believes all you've been feeding into it?'

Even without the short but descriptive oath he let fly with under his breath, Sheri knew she'd said too much, and in the wrong tone, just by the steely-eyed expression that came over his face. However, it was his hand snaking towards the door handle that caused her the most trepidation, and had her taking to her heels before she discovered just exactly what reprisal he had in mind!

From the safety of the verandah she heard the sound of the station wagon's engine start up, not without some relief—though grudgingly acknowledged—and with her lips pressed diffidently together she watched the vehicle's departure in moody contemplation.

Curiously, now that her emotions had cooled a little, it wasn't thoughts of her own behaviour that occupied her mind, but something even more unexpected. It was the first time in her life she could ever recall Roman being downright angry! She had seen him sarcastic, goading, even glacial on occasion, but not once had she seen him come close to really losing his temper—until a few minutes ago—and the fact that it had been herself who had incensed him enough to do so brought a frown of confusion to her forehead. She just couldn't fathom why such a distinction should apparently have been reserved for her alone.

Sheri had a splitting headache when she awoke later that morning—due, probably, to her having spent the majority of the intervening hours reliving the events of the previous evening—but which wasn't alleviated in the slightest by the almost reproachful glances her grandfather kept bestowing on her, or her mother's anticipated telephone call when it came. For not only was Heather already annoyed at there having been no one at home to receive her call the night before, but a chance remark by her father-in-law concerning Sheri and Roman was enough to bring down a torrent of recrimination, censure, and dogmatic instructions—all on the absent Todd's behalf—on to her daughter's head. Nor was Sheri's lot made any easier afterwards by her grandmother innocently enquiring whether she had anything planned for the day.

'Oh—er—I'm not sure really,' she stammered weakly in reply, and with the aid of a mouthful of water gulped down the two aspirins she'd just taken from a bottle. After last night it wouldn't have surprised her if Roman wanted nothing more to do with Chris's scheme—a thought she wholeheartedly supported!—but until she knew for certain she supposed she had to carry on as best she could, for her brother's sake at least. 'Roman did—did mention something about seeing me today, but ...' She shrugged, leaving it purposely vague.

'So you're going out with him again ... for the third day in a row!' her grandfather stated rather than questioned.

Sheri stared down selfconsciously at her hands. 'I guess so. If he comes,' she confirmed in a deprecating murmur.

'Do you really think that's a good idea?' gruffly.

'Well, of course it is if she likes him,' put in Beryl on a slightly exasperated note. 'In any event, I must say I rather like the young man myself.' Pausing, she sent her husband a wryly pointed glance. 'As I know you do too! You were only saying so a day or two before Sheri arrived ... remember?'

Colin shifted somewhat uncomfortably. 'Yes— well—that was in a completely different context,' he blustered. His voice firmed almost immediately. 'I certainly wasn't meaning as an escort for my only granddaughter!' And eyeing Sheri again, 'Anyway, what about this Todd, then, who's apparently waiting for you in Sydney?'

'Well, what about him?' countered Beryl promptly, before Sheri had time to open her mouth. 'They're not engaged or anything like that, so why shouldn't she see someone else if she wishes? The more so, I would have said, since there appears to be such a strong mutual attraction between her and Roman.' She patted her granddaughter's arm encouragingly. 'Isn't that right, love?'

Oh, hell, what had she started? Sheri despaired wretchedly. She had never intended to create any conflict between her grandparents—had never even imagined she might do so, in fact—and for all she knew she could be going through this for absolutely nothing if Roman did decide to leave her in the lurch, as it were. But until she knew for sure . . .

'Er—I suppose so,' she half smiled vaguely at her grandmother.

Not that Beryl seemed to find anything amiss, for she merely fixed her husband with a complacent look and stressed, 'There, you see!'

'All right, all right!' Expelling a disgruntled breath, Colin threw up his hands in mock surrender. 'If that's the way you're both determined to have it, then you won't hear any more arguments from me. Does that satisfy you?' He encompassed them both within his rather facetious regard before bending his head and getting on with his breakfast. Less than a minute later, though, he abruptly looked up again to warn, 'But his intentions had still better be honourable or I'll have plenty to say, believe me!'

Uncertain as to just how he meant that in view of his old-fashioned terminology, Sheri decided it was time to make her own standpoint quite clear.

'Grandpa, I only said I *liked* Roman . . . not that I was considering *marrying* him,' she said, ironically. And the former simply in order to help her brother!

'So what's that supposed to mean?' he took her aback by immediately frowning at her. 'That you're one of these so-called free spirits who prefers to indulge in uncommitted affairs rather than form a lasting relationship?'

'No, of course not!' she gasped, glad to be able to disabuse him of that idea at least. 'I merely meant that—that . . .' Oh, lord! Why hadn't she left well enough alone? She was only getting herself in deeper. With a gulp, she tried again. 'I merely meant that I'm finding his company quite enjoyable while I'm here, that's all.'

'It didn't look as if it was just his *company* you were enjoying last night,' he recalled significantly.

Sheri reddened selfconsciously, but fortunately her grandmother came to her rescue.

'Col, that's none of your business!' she scolded. 'If you're not careful you'll have Sheri regretting she returned to Goonagulla at all. These are the nineteen-eighties, you know, not the eighteen-eighties, and I'm sure she's quite capable of managing her own life without any interference from you. Besides,' she half smiled wryly, 'I thought you just said there would be no more arguments from you on the matter.'

'Hmm . . .' He acknowledged the reminder reluctantly, ruefully, but obviously still couldn't refrain from muttering, 'Things were different in my day.'

'Not *that* different,' retorted his wife drily. 'As I remember, my father had doubts at times regarding your intentions too, dear.' Half turning, she winked conspiratorially at Sheri. 'In those days your grandfather's reputation wasn't exactly what you would call spotless either.'

Colin looked away sheepishly. 'All the more reason for me to be concerned now,' he mumbled. 'I *know* what she's up against.'

'Well, well!' Sheri eyed him teasingly, relieved not to be the centre of attention any more. 'So it's your own guilty conscience that's been causing all your anxiety, is it, Grandpa?'

'Nothing of the kind!' he denied on a testy note, returning her gaze dourly from beneath beetling brows. 'I don't need to put my hand in the fire to know it's going to be burnt, do I?' His expression became artful. 'Something you might do well to remember, young lady.'

He wasn't wrong! 'I'll keep it in mind,' she averred wryly.

For the remainder of their meal the conversation turned to less contentious topics, so that by the time Sheri and her grandmother began clearing the table Colin's mood had relaxed considerably, and figuring the sooner she put in a good word for her brother's plans the sooner she would be able to avoid Roman's presence—that was, if he hadn't already taken the initiative from her yet again by deciding he'd had enough of her company!—Sheri made the most of her chance to raise the subject.

'Have you ever considered venturing into cotton, Grandpa?' she pretended to enquire first, carefully casual, but knowing full well what his answer would be.

'No, I haven't,' came his reply, as flat and succinct as she had expected.

'Why not?' she pressed on in the same negligent tone as she collected the last of the plates from the table and deposited them in the sink.

His features assumed a decidedly ironic mien. 'Because I'm quite content with the living we make from sheep.'

'You could do both, though, couldn't you? I mean
. . .' She stopped, not knowing whether it was prudent
to mention his neighbour's name again just at the
moment, then plunged on, 'Roman does, and very
successfully too, I gather.'

'So?' He leaned back in his chair, his eyes narrowed
watchfully.

Sheri hunched one shoulder in a deliberately
unconcerned movement. 'So I'm just surprised you
haven't also given it a try, that's all.'

'Why? Because now that you feel so friendly,' with a
sardonic inflection, 'towards Roman, you think that
whatever he does is automatically correct, or . . .
because Chris has told you about the idea he's
suddenly developed of wanting to follow suit?'

'Neither, actually,' she disclaimed with a quick
shake of her head, trying to avoid answering directly.
It obviously wouldn't do for him to suspect she had
already discussed the matter with her brother, but at
the same time she really didn't want to actually lie to
him either. 'I do manage to have some thoughts of my
own occasionally, you know.' A chafing edge made an
appearance in her own voice. More than once he too
had insinuated she only did as her mother commanded.
'It just seems to me it would be a good idea to
diversify.' She shrugged again.

'What makes you think we need to?'

'In these days of uncertain economics, if it isn't a
necessity, then it's at least judicious, isn't it?'

His bushy grey brows peaked satirically. 'So what
are you suggesting? That I should calmly give up all
I've worked for in order to allow Chris full rein?'

'Not at all,' she contradicted, and hiding a rueful
smile at his deliberate attempt to exaggerate the
matter. 'In fact, from what I hear, the grazing capacity
of the property needn't necessarily be diminished at

all, since a higher stocking rate would be attainable as a result of the permanent water available for irrigation of sown pastures.'

'Oh?' There was the definite sting of sarcasm in the questioning sound. 'Heard from whom? Roman, I suppose!'

'Well . . . yes,' Sheri admitted with a deprecating lift of her shoulders. 'I was discussing the subject with him on the way home last night, as it so happens.'

'The subject of *our* growing cotton!' her grandfather suddenly roared indignantly.

'No, no! The subject of *his* growing cotton, of course,' she corrected swiftly, conciliatorily. 'I was merely repeating what he said they'd found to be the case with regard to Castlewood.'

'And if that's what he said, then I'm sure it's correct,' inserted her grandmother abruptly from the sink where she was doing the washing up. 'Because Roman really knows what he's about when it comes to business. Doesn't he, Col?' She sought confirmation from her husband in a slightly humorous but firmly insistent tone.

For his part, Colin moved restively beneath her unswerving gaze for a few seconds before finally giving a defeated sigh. 'Mmm, he certainly knows what he's doing all right, as well as having the best feel for the way the market's likely to swing that I've seen in a long time,' he conceded. Then, in a return to his less tractable manner, 'That still doesn't mean I have to blindly copy whatever he does, though!'

'It doesn't mean you have to purposely oppose doing the same either,' Beryl retorted promptly. 'After all, Ellimatta isn't that much smaller than Castlewood, and if Chris is really keen to give it a go . . .'

'Perhaps you could . . . at least discuss it with him,' added Sheri, softly persuasive. 'You never know, you may even find you're in favour of the idea if you just talked about it for a little.'

'Even if he isn't, I still don't see that it's fair to completely deny Chris the chance to do as he wants,' Beryl declared, and received a long-suffering glare from her husband for her pains.

'Fair!' he barked exasperatedly. 'Running a property isn't supposed to be fair, woman! It's supposed to be profitable!'

Beryl simply smiled. 'And cotton isn't?' she quizzed subtly.

'Oh, of course it is! We all know that,' he had no option but to concur, even if in a vexed fashion.

'Then you will—as Sheri suggested—at least discuss it with him?'

Colin pulled irritably at his ear. 'I'm beginning to think it would be worthwhile . . . if only for the sake of some peace and quiet!'

Sheri drew in a sharp breath. Was he really implying what it sounded as if he might be? 'You mean it, Grandpa? You'll actually talk to Chris about it?' she sounded cautiously.

'I—well . . .' He half shrugged noncommittally, seemingly already regretting his impulsive remark, but his wife wasn't anywhere near so reticent.

'He will,' she stated unequivocally, fixing him with a challenging gaze.

And although he huffed and puffed a few moments longer, finally he relented. 'Oh, I suppose so,' he agreed grudgingly. 'Although I'm not promising anything, mind! So don't go thinking it's a foregone conclusion.'

'Naturally not,' Sheri was only too willing to allow. After all, her objective had only been to get him to the talking stage. Whatever happened from here was up to Chris. 'But by all accounts, I can't see anything but good coming from it.'

'Hmm . . .' The corners of his mouth turned down ironically as he rose to his feet, and noted the two pleased expressions opposite him with astute eyes. 'I wouldn't put it past the three of you—or should I make that four?' he inserted pointedly, looking in Sheri's direction, 'to have arranged this together,' he grumbled as he clumped from the room.

Fortunately for Sheri he didn't look back and so discover the guilty colour that immediately invaded her cheeks, but when she turned to begin drying another plate she did find her grandmother watching her in wry speculation.

'Well, was it?' Beryl queried.

'Arranged, you mean?' Sheri stalled for time in the hope of determining just how her grandmother was likely to react if told the truth.

'Mmm, that's precisely what I mean,' was the extremely drily voiced verification.

Which didn't exactly give away any clues! 'You did most of the convincing,' she continued to parry therefore.

'That's as may be,' Beryl granted, her lips curving obliquely. 'I just also happen to think the idea is a good one. Quite apart from considering Chris is entitled to give it a go if he wishes, and particularly since the place is as good as half his anyway.' Pausing, she held her granddaughter's gaze shrewdly. 'But the discussion was well and truly under way before I entered it, wasn't it? And knowing Chris as I do,' with an affectionate chuckle, 'I can't imagine him allowing any opportunity to slip through his fingers if it could possibly bring a little more pressure to bear on Col.'

Reassured somewhat by that small show of amusement, Sheri gave a rueful half smile in response. 'Yes, well, he did sort of mention that—er—any little help would be welcome,' she acceded.

Beryl nodded humorously. 'With Roman considerately supplying the appropriate information, I presume?'

'Er—more or less.'

Her grandmother nodded again. 'Just as I thought . . . and your grandfather suspects.'

That last addition had Sheri chewing at her lip anxiously. 'That won't have him changing his mind, though, will it?'

'Oh, I shouldn't think so. Not now he's actually committed himself this far,' Beryl reasoned comfortingly, and added, with a thoughtful pursing of her lips, 'Although to be on the safe side, I suppose it wouldn't hurt to ensure he doesn't get the chance to either.'

'How?'

'At a guess, I'd say by making certain he isn't provided with a reason to convert those suspicions into positive beliefs,' punctuated by an expressive laugh.

Since she at least had no intention of doing anything of the kind if she could possibly avoid it, Sheri continued with the drying up in a slightly easier frame of mind, but as ten o'clock approached, the supposed time of Roman's arrival, she found herself involuntarily tensing again, although for an entirely different reason.

Even if he did come, she didn't know what she was going to say to him—or him to her, which was probably more unsettling still. While if he didn't come at all she'd most likely feel no better, because although she might have felt relieved in the short term, in the long term she didn't doubt there would be as many of her grandfather's disconcerting questions to answer regarding Roman's sudden lack of interest as there had been concerning their original supposed involvement.

Altogether it was a worrying combination of

thoughts that had her rubbing miserably at her temples—the aspirins she'd taken earlier only having proved temporarily successful—and deciding on a walk in the fresh air in the hope that might produce the desired result.

Outside, the sun was warm on her back and she wandered aimlessly around the homestead for a while before beginning to amble down the track leading to the highway, knowing that if Roman did eventually come, and presumably via the Caldwells' as previously, she would still be able to hear his approach from where she was.

As it happened, however, the distant rumble of wheels she did pick up a short time later came from the direction in which she was heading, and chewing absently on a stalk of grass, she leant casually against the gate she had just come to, awaiting the vehicle's appearance with only mild interest.

That it should actually turn out to be Roman's station wagon caught Sheri unprepared and, swallowing apprehensively, she promptly felt her nerves tightening unbearably once more.

'Too anxious to see me to wait at the house, hmm?' was his drily mocking, opening remark as he pulled up on the other side of the gate.

Flushing slightly, she stared down at the grass stalk she had now begun to systematically shred with shaky fingers. 'I didn't even know if you were still coming,' she shrugged.

'I was certainly tempted not to.'

Without lifting her head, Sheri pressed her lips together and nodded, but didn't speak.

'However, I figured it was unfair to penalise Chris just because he had pigheaded relatives,' Roman's acidly drawling voice reached out to her again.

She did raise her head at that, but immediately

lowered it again on encountering the sardonic light in his vividly blue eyes. 'I'm sure he'll be very grateful,' she said stiffly. It was impossible for her to act normally when all his presence did was remind her of her mortifyingly unreserved behaviour the night before.

'Although you're not, I gather.'

'For being called pigheaded?' A small spark of resentment did surface then.

'That I came,' he clarified laconically.

'You said yourself, you considered not coming,' she countered with another diffident lifting of one shoulder.

He raked a hand through his thick hair roughly. 'Okay. If you've decided to give it a miss . . .' He re-started the car and put it into reverse.

Sheri took a step forward, as far as the gate permitted her to go, her eyes clouding doubtfully. 'You're leaving?' she questioned on a tentative note.

His mouth slanted wryly. 'I don't appear to be achieving much by staying here.'

'Oh—but . . .'

'Mmm . . .?' He flicked a well-shaped brow ironically high.

Sheri moistened her lips in a nervous movement. 'Wh-what about Chris?' she faltered.

'Well, what about him?' he returned, shrugging indifferently. 'I thought you'd just decided your pride was worth more than his plans.'

After all she'd done that morning in an effort to attain them! 'That's not true!' she rounded on him abruptly. 'Especially not in view of—in view of . . .' She stopped as unbidden tears put in an unwelcome, discomfiting appearance and she half turned away. She'd had enough of defending her actions for one morning!

'You do have a disconcerting habit of breaking off at the most interesting part of your sentences, don't you, sweetheart?' Roman drawled whimsically behind her. Quite close behind her, in fact, and a hasty look over her shoulder showed him to have left the car and to be nearing the gate with every lithe stride. 'Especially not in view of . . .?' he cued, resting tanned forearms on the top bar of the gate.

'Oh, go away, Roman!' she now flared contrarily, plaintively. 'I've already got a headache as it is. I don't need you making unfounded judgments, or getting your kicks by poking fun at me as well!'

In one agile movement he placed a hand on the gatepost and cleared the fence with ease. 'So what gave you the headache, princess?' he disregarded her latter complaints in order to probe first, to her surprise and no little consternation when he tipped her face up to his to scan her aggrieved features watchfully.

Since she had no intention of telling him the truth—that thoughts concerning him had been the initial cause—and since she was probably going to have to tell him some time what had occurred, anyway, Sheri settled for what had certainly done nothing to relieve it.

'The third degree I had to undergo this morning, I guess,' she sighed, even as she vainly attempted pulling away from the hand that still spanned her softly rounded chin.

'From Col?' he immediately wanted to know.

'And Mother. She rang this morning.' Her lips shaped ruefully. 'I think that must have set Grandpa off, though, because before that he was mostly contenting himself with just giving me highly reproachful glances . . . as if I'd just run over his best working dog.'

'Because of last night?' Roman deduced with a lazy smile.

Annoyed at both the way her heart pounded in

response to the attractive widening of his captivating mouth, and her cheeks flushed at the memory, Sheri merely nodded, not trusting herself to speak with anything like the offhandedness she wanted to portray.

'And the questions from your mother?' he half frowned curiously, although his lips still retained their beguiling upward curve. 'Don't tell me they were over the same thing.'

'O-only indirectly,' she stammered selfconsciously beneath his close gaze.

'How indirectly?' he quizzed swiftly, alertly.

'I told you at the Ball she wouldn't be in favour of my seeing you if she found out about it,' she said in a strengthening tone, and not without a hint of self-satisfaction at having been proved correct.

'Oh!' Releasing her at last, Roman suddenly gave a comprehending nod, a goading expression entering his eyes as they held hers. 'Been ordered home, have you?'

The aggravating look on his face had her temper rising ungovernably. 'Yes, as a matter of fact, I have!' she snapped.

'So when are you leaving?' he enquired in derisive tones.

Sheri's chin lifted to a defiant angle. 'Who said I was?'

'Isn't it inevitable? When Mother dictates . . . you obey?'

'No, it is not!' she found herself defending fiercely yet again. A deep, steadying breath, and she raised thickly lashed eyes mockingly to his. 'Otherwise I would be going home, *as instructed*, rather than remaining here, wouldn't I?'

Beneath their navy blue silk knit covering Roman's shoulders hunched indolently. 'Because your mother intends coming here instead?' he surmised, sarcasm uppermost. 'Or isn't even your insubordination sufficient to have her setting foot this far west again either?'

Back on the defensive once more, but on her parent's behalf this time, Sheri moved restlessly. 'That has nothing to do with it,' she claimed, though not particularly forcefully.

Roman uttered a scornful half laugh. 'Well, is she coming or isn't she?'

'N-no, she isn't, as it so happens,' she revealed both reluctantly and disappointedly. Not only because of her mother's apparently cavalier attitude towards Chris, but also because it confirmed both his and Roman's earlier prediction. 'She said that—that since Chris is clearly well on the road to complete recovery now, there really wasn't any n-necessity for her to make the trip, and—and particularly when there was some important work that needed her attention in Sydney.'

'Oh?' He gazed at her cynically askance. 'And what work would that be?'

'Ch-charity work,' Sheri disclosed jerkily.

Roman made a contemptuous sound deep in his throat. 'Something Heather obviously doesn't believe begins at home!'

'I guess not,' Sheri had little choice but to agree, her head lowering despondently.

'And is that the only reason you decided not to fall in with her wishes? Because she wouldn't be here to enforce them?'

The gibing note in his voice had her raising her head again immediately. 'No!' she grated infuriatedly, and in an effort to recover lost ground, forced a taunting look on to her face. 'The trouble with you is, you just don't appreciate how much my brother, and his aims, mean to me. That's the reason I'm still here, and why I've done my best to show how interested I am in preserving the ending of the feud!'

'In preserving the ending of the feud ... or in giving the impression you're interested in starting something else entirely?' Roman sought elucidation drily.

She could hardly deny it, but simultaneously, she wasn't about to divulge the true reason for her actions either. 'I—well, you didn't exactly go out of your way to dispel any thoughts Grandpa may have had regarding the latter last night, did you?' she countered tartly.

'I wouldn't have wanted him to think I was rejecting his only granddaughter's advances.' His lips twitched humorously.

'Except they didn't happen to be advances!' she denied hotly. 'I was merely playing a part!'

He tapped her goadingly beneath the chin he had recently held. 'But so convincingly,' he drawled in such an evocative manner that she had only too little trouble determining to just which occasion he was alluding.

Nevertheless, this time Sheri resolved he wouldn't put her on the defensive again—as had undoubtedly been his intention!—and she made herself smile archly at him, albeit between somewhat gritted teeth. 'Which just helps to prove my point, since by that I gather even you were beginning to labour under the same false impression,' she purred in distinctly mocking overtones, accompanied by a lightly amused laugh.

'Was I?' Roman's expression hardly altered in the slightest. His dark brows just flicked fractionally higher as his head tilted to one side in a considering gesture. 'Somehow I don't think so.'

About to offer a chafing assurance, Sheri wasn't given an opportunity to do anything of the kind because it seemed she had misinterpreted his reaction completely. Before she could rectify her mistake, she found herself swept into an embrace from which there was no escape and her lips possessed by a relentlessly exacting mouth that she knew all too disquietingly could be devastatingly accomplished in its effect.

Nor was it any less galvanising now, she discovered in a panic, despite all her desperate resolutions that it be otherwise. Steadily and surely she could feel her defences weakening as her unruly senses took charge, and of its own volition her traitorous body moved closer to the virile muscularity of his. Total capitulation was only a matter of time, she realised in an agony of despair, but still she seemed incapable of preventing the humiliating outcome, and finally, with a moan of defeat, she began returning the tantalising pressure with unrestrained fervour.

Then just as suddenly as he had claimed them, Roman now set her lips free. 'As I said . . . somehow I don't think so,' he repeated with just enough of a sardonic smile playing about his mouth to have Sheri's already heightened emotions spilling over into anger. It didn't matter that his breathing was almost as unsteady as her own; she just wanted to retaliate, and with that end in mind she swung a hand towards his lean, bronzed cheek with all the force she could muster.

'You contemptible, conceited swine!' she slated fiercely.

On this occasion her fingers never reached their target, however, because Roman swiftly arrested them in mid-air with an inflexible grip about her wrist. 'While you, sweetheart, are a troublesome, lying virago!' he returned with equal pungency as he yanked her unceremoniously to his side. 'If you're not

damned careful you'll give the game away altogether
with antics like that!' His fingers moved, digging deep
into her slender waist to ensure she stayed put. 'Either
Col or Beryl is at the front window and looking this
way.'

Diverted for the moment, Sheri glanced in the
direction of the homestead. 'It's Grandma,' she said
on recognising the patch of pale green visible in the
distance.'

'Then wave,' he ordered peremptorily.

'What for?' She cast a rebellious look upwards.

'So she knows you're leaving, and with whom,' he
answered, raising his own arm in a salute that was
promptly reciprocated by the figure at the window.

'Who said I was going anywhere with you?' she
demanded resentfully.

'I did!' she was informed succinctly, and had her
own arm propelled upwards so that she had no option
but to continue the movement and signal her
grandmother as directed. 'Want to make something of
it?'

Sheri's first impulse was to hurl a defiant
affirmation at him, but there was something in his set
expression that made her think twice about the
advisability of such an action, and in the end prudence
won out.

'Not particularly,' she conceded with a grimace.

Roman's white teeth gleamed in a sudden, unanticipated grin. 'I'm glad to hear it. You would've
lost,' he drawled as he opened the gate.

'Because you can always resort to physical force if
all else fails?' she gibed, storming past him with her
head lifted high

Roman closed the gate again and caught up to her at
the car. 'You mean, in the same way you did a moment
ago?' he queried.

Sheri flounced on to the front seat and jerked the door shut. 'You deserved it!' she smouldered.

His brows shot skywards mockingly as he slid his long length in beside her. 'Because you don't know your own mind?'

Not unnaturally, the treacherous reaction his kisses brought about within her wasn't a subject she cared to pursue, and with a haughty sniff she turned to stare out of the window when, with a last wave to her grandmother, he set the station wagon in motion.

'Well, at least it would appear Beryl has no qualms about our—er—continuing association,' he commented in wry accents.

'Why would she?' Her lips formed a caustic moue as she partly glanced his way. 'She seems to be suffering under the illusion that I've suddenly discovered the man of my dreams.' She gave a lightly taunting laugh. 'It's amazing what some people will believe, isn't it?'

'Uh-huh,' he concurred lazily, but with such a subtle nuance in his tone that she immediately suspected his reply had nothing whatsoever to do with her grandmother's beliefs. 'Although in Beryl's case I guess you can hardly blame her since your actions, in *public* at least,' with satirical emphasis, 'have certainly done nothing to discourage such thinking.'

'Not for that reason, though!' she burst out hastily. She didn't want him thinking there might have been a grain of truth in her grandmother's imaginings, and definitely not in view of her wayward responses each time he'd kissed her! 'I merely thought—for Chris's sake, of course,' she interposed self-protectively, 'that it would help to make the—er—united front the pair of you wanted impressed upon Grandpa so much appear more feasible, that's all. They each made their own deductions from there.' Which wasn't quite the way of it, but certainly what she wanted the man beside her to think.

Roman assimilated the information with a sceptical twitch of his lips. 'Each?' he promptly questioned alertly.

'Mmm, that's right.' Sheri granted herself the luxury of a mocking smile as she pictured the sudden consternation her next intended disclosure would doubtless produce. 'You see, being somewhat old-fashioned in his outlook, it seems Grandpa may now be envisioning us married off already.'

To Sheri's utter disappointment, as well as no little surprise, not one iota of the annoyance or dismay she had expected became evident. 'Is he now?' Roman merely drawled and flicked her a provoking glance. 'I sure wasn't wrong when I said the Taylors were a contrary breed, was I?'

Considering events as a whole, Sheri didn't really feel she was in any position to deny the charge right at present, regardless of how much it irritated. Instead she made the best of it by smiling secretively and claiming, 'Fortunately for you, perhaps.'

'Oh?' She had the pleasure of seeing his blue eyes narrow watchfully within their ebony frames. 'In what way?'

Stretching comfortably in her seat, she decided to keep him in suspense a little longer. 'Well, I don't suppose you'll have to worry about the gates suddenly being locked any more now, will you?'

'If I'd known that, I could have saved myself some considerable time by coming through Newhaven again this morning, but as it was, I thought it a fair bet Col would have been out bright and early to close that entrance off too,' Roman divulged wryly, and concurrently explaining why he had chosen the longer route via the main road. 'However . . .' he went on in a slow but significant drawl, 'I suspect that wasn't quite what you were inferring originally.' He paused, sending her a speaking glance. 'Was it, sweetheart?'

She shrugged noncommittally. 'What makes you think that?'

'For starters, your insufferably smug expression, I expect!' His retort came in exceedingly dry tones.

From smug to goading was only a short step and Sheri accomplished it in very short order as she waved a remonstrating finger at him. 'Uh-uh! Flattery will get you nowhere,' she quipped.

'So what will? My stopping the car?' he half threatened.

'In order that you can browbeat me without distraction?' Her eyes widened mockingly. 'Somehow I don't think that would achieve very much either.'

'Neither do I.' The wide sweep of his mouth curved ruefully. 'Although probably only because it isn't your brow I consider needs beating!'

'Oh, good heavens! Male chauvinism at its most rampant!' she chided in bantering tones. She was starting to enjoy having him at a disadvantage for a change. 'First flattery, and now threats. What will be next, I wonder?' Tapping a forefinger against her chin in a gesture of assumed speculation.

Now Roman did bring the vehicle to an abrupt halt. 'Something you may find even less palatable than the first two, if you don't watch yourself!' he taunted as he whipped a hand out to grasp the nape of her neck. 'So now I suggest you cut the stalling and start talking. And don't you dare ask, "About what?"' he anticipated, giving her an accentuating shake, 'because you already know damned well what about. Now *give*!'

Sheri sighed sorrowfully, surmising she'd pushed him as far as he was going to go. 'Oh, well, if you insist,' she acquiesced, but with every evidence of regret. 'You're fortunate Grandpa has changed his mind, because I suspect he may not have otherwise been so receptive to other suggestions.' She still couldn't quite forgo making her reply as enigmatic as possible.

Successfully too, it appeared, judging by Roman's frowning expression as he probed closely, 'Such as?'

'Which do you suppose?' she tried to shrug, straight-faced, but a telltale smile of triumph began pulling at the edges of her mouth.

Roman's frown became tinged with a look of disbelief. 'Are you telling me . . . in as roundabout way as possible, of course,' he inserted ironically, 'that at long last he's finally agreed to discuss Chris's plans for growing cotton?'

Sheri pretended to give the matter some thought. 'Mmm, that's about the gist of it, I guess,' she eventually confirmed in whimsical accents.

'And you've known all this time without telling me? You devious little witch!' he both half laughed and shook her at the same time. 'How the hell did you get him to agree to that so quickly?'

'By sheer brilliance, actually,' she dimpled. His obvious good humour and pleasure were infectious. As was the manner in which his fingers were now toying absently with the strands of her brightly coloured hair at the side of her neck, she found with another of those unpredictable surges of awareness. 'However, to be strictly honest, I can't really take all the credit,' she continued less facetiously, 'because Grandma was the one who extracted the actual agreement from him. Apparently she feels it's only fair Chris be allowed to at least give it a try. I more or less just set the ball in motion.'

'That's still a lot more than either Chris or I were able to do,' he credited, his lazily curving mouth taking on a wry slant.

'Due, no doubt, to your obviously only trying when Grandma was absent,' she deduced with a grin. 'And thereby underestimating the influence a wife is able to exert on her husband at times.' Her green eyes glinted mockingly.

'As well as a certain provoking redhead?' he countered drily.

'Me?' Her expression was all innocence. 'But I don't have a husband.'

Roman's mouth sloped crookedly. 'More's the pity, I'm beginning to think.'

'Can't take the pressure, huh?' she couldn't resist gibing. Maybe her earlier disclosure had got to him after all.

'Is that a challenge?' Metallic blue eyes fastened inescapably to hers.

Sheri swallowed nervously but kept her tone unconcerned. 'To do what?'

'Take you on at your own game, perhaps?'

'Except as I've said before . . . I don't happen to *be* playing any game.'

'Mmm, so you did,' he concurred with a cynical indolence that had her deciding it might have been an auspicious time to return to their original topic.

'Oh, well, at least Chris should be pleased when he hears the news,' she shrugged.

'Extremely so, I imagine. As well as deeply grateful, no doubt,' he declared with an unexpected tinge of dryness that had Sheri's eyes shading confusedly—oh, lord, he hadn't guessed at those feelings of disquiet that had abruptly assailed her, had he?—but which quickly vanished on hearing his ensuing suggestion. 'So how about we drive in to town and tell him about it, hmm?' He bent to turn the ignition switch, anticipating her acceptance.

An endorsement that came readily. 'Oh, yes, I'm sure he'd like to know as soon as possible,' she agreed. And wanting to keep the uncomplicated conversation flowing, 'It will help cheer him up. I think he's been finding time dragging by excruciatingly slowly this last couple of days now that he's started to feel so much better, and it's obvious he's just champing at the bit to get home again.'

'Well, what he's about to hear should definitely give his spirits a lift until that happens. It's supposed to be some time this week, isn't it?'

'Mmm, Wednesday or Thursday as far as I know,' she confirmed, smiling pleasurably at the thought. She was looking forward to being able to spend a little more time with her only brother. It was an opportunity they normally had only rarely.

Roman spared her a fleeting, interested glance as he concentrated on his driving once more. 'While we're on the subject of Chris, though . . . what did you think of Howard Arthur's news this morning?'

Sheri stared at him perplexedly. She knew Howard Arthur was the local police sergeant, but she certainly had no knowledge of him imparting any news. 'I don't know. What news is that?' she frowned.

'You mean he still hasn't been able to get through to you?' he queried in surprise. 'You must have had a very busy line this morning. He said he'd already tried twice before he rang me but you were engaged each time.'

'Probably with Mother.' An expressive grimace appeared momentarily. 'But what news?' she asked again, a touch of anxiety creeping into her tone.

'That they've got the bloke who shot Chris,' he disclosed in clipped accents.

Taken completely unawares by the information, it took her a second or two to absorb it, but once she had done so, a flurry of questions poured forth. 'But how? I thought you said there was no one around at the time. And when? Was he a local, or someone from out of town? Do you know him?'

Having waited patiently for her to finish, Roman cast her an oblique look. 'You want those answered in order, or just as they come to mind?' he drawled, amusement paramount.

Sheri bit at her lip ruefully. 'As they come to mind will do.'

'That's a relief,' he half grinned before complying. 'But no, I don't know him, because I'm glad to say he isn't a local. That sort we can do without!' he added with graphic feeling. 'I gather he's just a young lout in town for a couple of weeks with a few of his mates, looking to do a spot of shooting, and decided Ellimatta seemed as good a place as any to try their luck.'

'And did he know he'd shot someone?' she asked quietly.

'Oh, yes, he knew all right, but apparently they believed Chris had been killed outright, and so they cleared off the place as fast as they could in a panic. The gutless bastards!' he swore with such contempt that Sheri didn't doubt they would have received very rough justice if Roman had managed to locate them at the time of the shooting.

'So how did the police discover who'd done it, then?' she probed.

He made a derisive sound. 'As a result of the fellers' own cowardice! For although they may have departed Ellimatta at a rate of knots, they just weren't game enough to leave town with the same dispatch in case it drew unwanted attention to themselves when they least needed it. It seems they'd only arrived two days before and had spent just about the whole of the intervening period bragging about the shooting they were planning on doing during the next couple of weeks. Naturally, they thought it might appear somewhat odd if they then suddenly skipped town on the very day someone was shot, so they decided it would be smarter just to keep a low profile until they were due to leave. Nevertheless, the fact that, after all their talking, they weren't going out and doing any shooting either had some of their previous listeners wondering, and one of them happened to mention something of the sort to Howard. He thought it worth investigating, and the chap who actually shot Chris broke down and confessed while he was being questioned.'

'I see,' she sighed thoughtfully, but thankful at least that the man had been caught. 'Chris will doubtless be pleased to hear that news too ... as well as Grandma and Grandpa. Although Grandpa's tried to conceal it, I think the thought that the culprit hadn't been caught and therefore might possibly pay another visit to the property has been giving him some worries.'

'To add to those concerning his granddaughter?' Roman surmised drily.

Sheri gave a selfconscious shrug. 'Yes, well, in that regard, I suppose there's really no need for you and me to keep up this pretence any longer now that he's actually agreed to discuss Chris's plans with him. And I expect you'd rather make your peace with—with Nerissa as soon as possible too.' Oddly, she now found the idea more than a little dispiriting.

Roman's gaze slanted over her wryly. 'All in good time, sweetheart, all in good time,' he drawled— mockingly, she thought. 'However, I wouldn't be in too much of a hurry to bring our association to an end, if I were you. Col's no fool, and if he should suspect he's been set up, then we could well see not only Chris's hopes being summarily squashed, but the feud back on for another hundred years as well!'

'That's what Grandma more or less insinuated,' she allowed herself to own.

His dark head inclined lazily. 'A wise woman, your grandmother, it seems.'

'I guess she must be,' Sheri conceded as she relaxed again, feeling strangely content. Not only had her headache abruptly disappeared, but in spite of its unpromising beginnings she suddenly felt it wasn't going to turn out to be such a disaster of a day after all.

CHAPTER SEVEN

To say Chris had been pleased with the news he received regarding his grandfather's decision was an understatement. Jubilant would probably have been closer to the mark, coupled with a very real relief because it was patently clear to his sister that he considered his most difficult obstacle had now been overcome and that it would be only a matter of time before the actual work on the new venture could begin.

However, no matter how confident he was of his ability to convince his grandfather of the viability of the project, Sheri still wasn't prepared for the sight which met her eyes when checking the fences in the Five Mile Paddock on her grandparent's behalf the day after Chris arrived home from the hospital.

The first inkling she had that all wasn't as it should be was when she picked up the sound of heavy machinery, noticeable even over the engine of her bike, coming from beyond an intervening stand of trees as she neared the appropriate gate, but on passing through and skirting the timber she could only bring the bike to a sudden stop as she stared, aghast, at the scene before her. The paddock was already being pulled and burnt! she realised with a shocked gasp.

To her left a tracked earth mover, a bulldozing blade attached to the front and a set of ripping tines on the back, was systematically disposing of everything in its path, while towards the now barren centre of the paddock three or four piles of uprooted trees and assorted vegetation were being reduced to smouldering embers.

With a furious intake of breath, Sheri dragged her hat down more securely on to her waving russet hair, opened up the bike's throttle, and set off for the alien machine at top speed. Apparently the driver must have seen her coming, because the machine had already come to a halt before she reached it, a disturbingly familiar long-legged figure jumping lithely to the ground from the cabin to lean negligently against the blade as she slewed to rest in front of him.

'Just what the hell do you think you're doing, Roman?' she demanded indignantly as she swung off the bike.

His eyes scanned the paddock slowly and returned to rest tauntingly on her resentful features. 'Isn't it obvious?' he drawled. 'Or has it been so long, since you've—er—decided to live elsewhere that you've forgotten how land's cleared?'

Sheri's breathing accelerated rapidly as a result of the two purposely nettling remarks. 'No, I haven't forgotten, and where I live has nothing to do with it!' she flared. 'How dare you come in here and start working our land!'

'Chris is hardly in a position to do so,' he said drolly.

'And I've only your word for it that he would want to!' she immediately sniped. 'Grandpa said he was willing to *discuss* the idea, nothing else, so you can get off this property right now!'

'On *your* orders?' His well-shaped brows reached an eloquent peak.

Sheri glared at him, incensed. 'That's right, on *my* orders!' she gritted. 'Even though I may only be a visitor at the moment, I do still happen to be a Taylor, you know!'

Easing himself slowly upright, Roman tapped her

cheek goadingly. 'But not one with any rights concerning the running of this property, I believe.'

'Enough to order a trespasser off, though!'

'Except I don't happen to be trespassing,' he pointed out in a secretly amused tone that had her hands clenching involuntarily at her sides. 'I'm here on request.'

'That's a likely story!' she grimaced disbelievingly.

'A damn sight more likely than my doing this uninvited because I had nothing better to do!' he retorted, heavily sarcastic now.

Sheri chewed discomfitedly at her lower lip. If she didn't allow him to antagonise her to such an extent she would probably have realised that for herself. 'Well, why are you here, then?' she queried on a more diffident note.

His lips sloped obliquely. 'As I said ... because I was requested to make a start on the clearing.'

'By ... Chris?' she hazarded, frowning. 'It could only have been him, couldn't it?'

'Uh-huh,' came the laconic verification.

'Because he considers Grandpa's approval a foregone conclusion?'

'That, and the fact that if he doesn't begin preparing the ground now it won't be ready in time for next season's planting. Which means, of course, that he'll have wasted another year.'

Despite being able to understand her brother's apparent point of view, for once Sheri found herself unable to agree with him. 'Well, I still don't think he should be going ahead with it behind Grandpa's back,' she declared defiantly. 'It's not fair, and—and if he's so sure Grandpa will approve, why can't he wait until then? He's home now, so they can discuss it any time. Surely another week or so wouldn't make any difference?'

'Wouldn't it?' Roman eyed her sardonically. 'Then you obviously aren't aware just how much work is required to prepare this paddock. It doesn't finish once it's cleared, sweetheart. Before it can even be ploughed it has to be accurately graded to ensure the levels are correct for irrigation, plus the water channels themselves still have to be excavated, and it all takes time, I can assure you.'

'I don't care!' she defended. 'I . . .'

'No, why should you?' he cut in on a satirical note. 'It will be no skin off your nose if it's not completed on schedule. You'll be back in Sydney by then and once again totally unconcerned with whatever's happening out here!'

'That's not the point!' she retorted vexedly. She still neither needed nor wanted his unwarranted opinions! 'Even if it was true, which it isn't,' she felt obliged to add, albeit a trifle querulously. 'I just don't think it's right, that's all.' She paused, her expression assuming a more challenging cast. 'Anyway, what if Grandpa *doesn't* approve? What's he going to say about all this, then?' She flung a hand wide to indicate the almost completely denuded area surrounding them.

Surprisingly, that had the broad curve of his mouth sweeping upwards into a wide, engaging smile, and to her irritation her own pulse increasing rapidly as a result. 'Well, whatever it is, I've no doubt we'll be able to hear it all the way to Castlewood,' he predicted humorously.

Her own unruly reaction to that smile, as much as his words, had Sheri's anger returning. 'And you've got the hide to accuse me of not caring what happens!' she charged fierily. 'It seems to me the shoe's on the other foot! If there is any trouble, you'll be safely out of the way on your own place while Chris takes the brunt of Grandpa's fury, when all the time it will have been you who did all the damage!'

Unperturbed, Roman's smile didn't falter in the slightest. 'And in the unlikely event that there is any trouble, I'm sure Col will make certain that no one who had a part in it is allowed to escape the lash of his tongue,' he deduced in a dry voice. 'Nonetheless, and whatever the outcome, at least I'll know my actions were dictated by a desire to assist your brother . . . and not as yours appear to be, my sweet,' in a bitingly mocking tone, 'out of pure obstructiveness . . . as always!'

Oh, so now she was obstructive too, was she? Along with all the other faults he'd denouced her as having! Sheri seethed. Well, on this occasion she just felt inclined enough to prove him right for once!

'Because I said I thought you shouldn't be clearing the land yet?' she made herself enquire calmly. Then, while he was still unsuspecting, she leapt on to the machine's track to enable her to reef the key from the ignition, along with its connected companions, and hurled them as far as she could into the distance. Watching, she saw them clear the boundary fence, bounce once on the lip of one of Castlewood's own irrigation channels before disappearing from view down its side, and she gulped. Actually she hadn't intended to make them quite that inaccessible, but since they were she didn't mind taking advantage of the fact. 'Well, now you can't continue, can you?' she taunted smugly as she dusted her hands together and looked down at the man below her.

'You bloody little . . .!' Roman stifled a rasped epithet as he took a quick step towards her, his demeanour ominously threatening. 'Well, now *you* can just go and get them again!'

Ensuring her graceful jump to the ground was

executed a protectively safe distance away from him,
Sheri gave a defiant shake of her head. 'I'm not getting
them. They're your keys,' she declared with as much
nonchalance as she could gather. Truth to tell, the
implacable look on his face had her feeling just a mite
apprehensive at the moment.

'And some of which happen to be quite important!'
she was informed on a stony note.

'In that case, I won't delay your retrieving them,'
she shrugged with creditable indifference and, making
the most of the opportunity, began heading for her
bike with alacrity.

'Oh, no, you don't!' Her progress was abruptly
halted when Roman caught hold of her arm with
inescapable fingers, the accompanying smile he
bestowed on her this time more menacing than
engaging. 'You put them in there, sweetheart,' there
was absolutely nothing endearing, or even teasing, in
the word, just sheer stinging abrasiveness, 'so you get
them out!' He began propelling her determinedly
towards the fence.

'I will not!' she shouted, struggling furiously against
his restraining hold. 'Why should I? It's your fault
they're . . .'

'Listen, my sweet!' he interrupted with biting
acrimony as he simultaneously brought them to a
sudden stop and took hold of her chin in an immobilising
hand. 'Let's get this quite clear, because you've got two
choices only. Either you get in there and look for them
under your own steam, or I'll damned well throw you
in!' His head lowered, his ebony-lashed eyes locking
relentlessly with hers. 'And believe me, right at present
I'm not real fussy which one it is!'

Sheri jerked her head away resentfully from his
disquieting touch. 'No, why should you be?' she
gibed. 'Brute force is a handy weapon to have at your

disposal, isn't it? Especially against someone considerably weaker than yourself!'

Reaching the fence, Roman swung her over it in an effortless movement, much to her annoyance, then cleared it himself with equal ease. 'Perhaps you should have remembered that before contemplating such a senseless action,' he mocked.

'How was I to know you were going to be such a louse about it?' she flared defensively, followed by a grimace on seeing the stretch of water in the channel before her. 'Besides,' her tone turned disgruntled, 'I didn't mean to throw them in here. I was aiming for those bushes.' Indicating the scrubby growth a few yards further along the fence.

'Then you should also have been more careful, shouldn't you?' he countered unsympathetically. 'Meanwhile, however . . .' A significant glance was directed towards the water.

Sheri bit at her lip doubtfully, searching his face for even the smallest sign that he might relent. 'You're not really going to make me get in there, are you?'

'As I said, you've got two choices . . .'

'But I don't even know exactly where they went in!' she wailed.

'No?' His brows arched with utter unconcern. 'Well, once you find them, you will.'

Realising she was making no impression on him at all and that his attitude was as unyielding as ever, Sheri sent him a baleful glare and lowered herself to the ground to begin dragging off her riding boots and socks. But after rolling up the legs of her jeans to her knees and gingerly starting to inch down the smooth, hard baked edge of the channel, she couldn't help but give some vent to her feelings.

'Ruthless, unfeeling rat!' she disparaged to herself in a mutter.

'Capricious, scheming tartar!' came the immediate retaliation, advising she'd still been overheard.

Tartar! Indignation had her swivelling round impulsively, intent on delivering a withering retort, but on such a steep slope the action was an injudicious one that promptly had her overbalancing and sliding helplessly the rest of the way into the water. Struggling to her feet again a few seconds later, all thoughts of taking Roman to task had been temporarily banished as she glanced down at her now saturated clothing and part lamented, part complained, 'Oh, now look at me!'

From his position on the bank where he was squatting on his haunches, Roman grinned impenitently. 'Mmm ... and very nice too,' he drawled, his eyes surveying her dripping figure leisurely.

Suddenly conscious that for all the protection her clinging shirt was affording her she might as well have been standing there naked, Sheri's face flamed with embarrassment. 'Oh! You—you ...!' she began wrathfully, and bending down sought not only to deprive him of the view she presented, but also in the hope of finding something, anything, on the channel bed that she could throw at him. Eventually her groping fingers connected with something metal and she grabbed at it exultantly, only to find as she brought it to the surface that it was the very object she had been seeking. Still, it was better than nothing. 'There!' she exclaimed, hurling the key-ring towards the figure above her as hard as she could. 'You've got your damned keys back! Now I hope you're satisfied!'

'Thanks.' He caught them deftly, to her disappointment, and rising agilely to his feet started for the fence.

Sheri expelled an aggrieved breath as she watched

him for a moment, then dropped her gaze to the slope
confronting her. The miserable heel surely didn't
expect her to try and clamber up there again on her
own! The thought that he might had her opening her
mouth quickly.

'Roman!' she called half angrily, half reproachfully.

In time—his own time! she noted, glowering—he
reappeared to stand with his hands resting casually on
lean hips as he looked down at her. 'Mmm . . .?'

Her emerald eyes flashed stormily as a result of his
deliberate obtuseness. 'You might at least give me a
hand out!'

'I thought you objected to my seeing you in such—
er—revealing circumstances.' His lips twitched aggravatingly.

Considering her predicament, Sheri had no choice
but to clamp down on her feelings as best she could.
She wasn't really in a position to take issue with him
about either his attempt to disconcert her or his
obvious amusement at the situation. 'I object even
more to remaining here,' she declared instead. 'This
water's not as warm as it could be.'

To her relief he at last condescended to bend down
and extend a hand towards her—but only so far. 'So
what do you say?' he prompted on a goading note.

It would have been all manner of uncomplimentary
things if the circumstances had been different, but
while he was so obviously in command she could only
comply. 'Please!' she heaved.

Leaning further down, Roman caught hold of her
hand in a firm grasp, although he still didn't
immediately exert any leverage. 'And for throwing
these away?' He gave a meaningful tap to his shirt
pocket.

Sheri could only glare at him impotently. 'All right,
I'm sorry!' she flared on a choking note. Then bitterly,

when she was safely, finally, standing beside him,
'You really like your pound of flesh, don't you?'

With a lazy smile he brushed a hand along the
underside of her jaw. 'And when it's such attractive
flesh . . . why not?'

To her chagrin this time Sheri couldn't control her
feelings and her face became suffused with colour once
again as she took a swift step backwards. 'Because you
might at least *pretend* to some courteous instincts!' she
sniped.

One corner of his shapely mouth quirked humorously. 'Such as, offering you my shirt, you mean?'

'Oh, go to hell!' she promptly blazed. The idea that
he was merely amusing himself at her expense was
unbearably irritating. 'I wouldn't accept your shirt
even in the highly unlikely event that you did offer it.
There'd probably be conditions attached to my
accepting it!' Bending quickly to retrieve her boots and
socks, she began making for the fence with her head
held at a haughty angle.

For the second time that morning, though, she had
only managed to take a couple of steps before she was
brought to a halt with a hand on her arm.

'Not so fast, princess,' Roman counselled drily,
spinning her back to face him. 'I wanted a word with
you, anyway.' He indicated the grass beside the fence.
'So how about we sit down, huh?'

'No, thanks.' Sheri gave a disdainful shake of her
head. 'I can't imagine anything we need to discuss,
and besides,' as a not altogether truthful afterthought
came to mind, 'I'm starting to feel cold.'

'Then sitting in the sun will undoubtedly warm you
faster than a ride back to the homestead on your bike,'
he proposed in wry tones, lowering himself to the
ground, and by virtue of the hold he still had on her
relentlessly forced her into doing the same.

With her breasts heaving, Sheri cast him a peeved glare. 'Well?' she demanded impatiently when he didn't immediately speak.

Relinquishing his grip, Roman indolently re-settled his ever-present bush hat on his head. 'Col wouldn't have been up to his old tricks again yesterday, by any chance, would he?' was his whimsically voiced and startling enquiry that had Sheri momentarily forgetting her indignation and staring at him in bewilderment.

'I don't know what you mean,' she frowned. 'What tricks?'

'Oh, you know the type of thing. A gate left open here, a fence cut there, stock released from holding yards, etcetera.'

Suddenly realisation came to her. 'But that was during the feud!' she exclaimed. 'And—and in any case, your family weren't exactly backward in doing the same to us!'

'True.' His blue eyes filled with unremorseful laughter. 'But that was also before we agreed to a truce.'

'Well, so did Grandpa!'

'Mmm, but somewhat less than enthusiastically.' He stopped, sending her an ironic look. 'And we both know what his feelings are concerning our association, don't we?'

'Well . . . y-yes,' she faltered. Then, recovering, 'Not that I can see what that's got to do with anything. I mean, the last time he actually mentioned the subject to me he was talking in terms of honourable intentions . . . remember?' Her winged brows rose to a mocking peak.

'How could I forget?' he returned in a sardonic drawl, and unaccountably had her experiencing a discomfiting sense of depression. 'Although, at the same time, maybe that was simply an expedient way to cover his own intentions.'

'No!' Sheri disallowed immediately, loyally, an impatient hand sweeping back drying strands of hair from her face. 'Grandpa wouldn't do anything like that, and especially not when he's given his word!'

Roman looked slightly less believing. 'Although he *was* out in the back paddock yesterday, wasn't he?'

Twin furrows made an appearance above her tiptilted nose. 'Well, yes—twice, as a matter of fact,' she confirmed uneasily. Chris and herself had laughed about it at the time, actually. 'He wanted to use the back road to visit Leo Weymark,' a neighbour some ten miles distant, 'but he'd forgotten he'd put locks on the gates, and as he didn't have the keys with him he had to come back for them.'

'Which wouldn't have done much to improve his disposition, of course,' drily.

'No, he was as mad as a wet hen about it, as it so happens,' she confessed a little wryly. 'Not that that means he'd take his annoyance out on you, though, if that's what you're implying!' Her indignation began returning in full force.

'No?' His firmly chiselled mouth crooked expressively. 'Well, when you've put up with as much of your grandfather's nonsense as we have over the years, and for equally irrelevant reasons, you may just find yourself becoming as sceptical as we are on that point.'

Sheri's head lifted defiantly. 'I doubt it! And as I said, particularly not since he's agreed to a truce.' Pausing, she slanted him a cautious, sidelong glance. 'What's he supposed to have done, anyway?' she probed on a slightly defensive note.

'Nothing especially calamitous, as it turned out, just damned time-consuming,' he revealed in an irritated tone. 'Hayden and I spent the whole of yesterday afternoon mustering a mob of sheep which had spread to just about every corner of the Shire as a result of the gate to our own back paddock having been thoughtfully opened!'

'And just because Grandpa happened to use the same road you're accusing him of doing it!' she expostulated in disbelief. 'Why, it could have been anyone who opened the gate! Or even either of you not shutting it properly, if it comes to that!'

'Except that it wasn't one of us, but it *is* the type of antic Col's had a penchant for in the past!' he retorted. 'As you doubtless can recall.' His eyes held hers meaningfully.

'Yes, but as you just mentioned, that was in the past!' she tried impressing on him, since she was as aware as he was that she couldn't deny it. 'Besides, it could have been another group of shooters, just like the ones who came on to Ellimatta without asking.'

'Uh-uh!' he vetoed with decisive assurance. 'There were no new tracks going through the gateway. That's what made it so suspicious.'

Sheri could understand how it would, but at the same time she wasn't about to allow such circumstantial evidence to diminish her own belief in her grandfather. 'That still doesn't mean Grandpa did it, though!' she maintained in a steadfast voice. And especially not after him agreeing to end the feud! That was the main stumbling block as far as she was concerned. Abruptly, a stray thought emerged and she sent the man beside her a speculative glance. 'Unless, of course, *if* he did do it,' stressed insistently, 'it was only because he considered you'd broken the truce first.'

Roman uttered a scornful laugh, shaking his head. 'Oh, come on, sweetheart! Broken the truce doing what?' he quizzed mockingly. 'You know damned well we've done nothing of the kind, if only for the fact that you obviously aren't aware of what it could be, and knowing Col of old, I very much doubt he'd keep something of that nature to himself. He'd be raging about it to all and sundry, and you know that too!'

Sheri exhaled dismally. That was another point she couldn't dispute. 'Well, why do you think he'd do it, then? If he did do it.' She still wasn't going to meekly assume he'd been the culprit.

Roman rubbed a hand ruefully around the back of his neck. 'As I said, maybe he's decided it's the best way to ... protect his granddaughter, or maybe it's just a case of old habits dying hard.' Halting, his lips curved satirically. 'The more so when they were as ingrained as they were in Col, and he used to get such a kick out of them when they were successful.'

Sheri gave a helpless grimace. She wished he wouldn't keep making points she hadn't a hope of denying, because she could recollect all too vividly the devilish delight her grandfather had displayed on so many such occasions. Although he hadn't yesterday, she suddenly recalled, her spirits rising, and surely that must prove something!

'Then why didn't he show the same enjoyment yesterday?' she triumphantly asked as much of Roman. 'Why did we only get to hear complaints regarding the nuisance the locks had caused him?'

'Because he's supposed to be abiding by a truce ... remember?' His reply was strongly laced with acid irony. 'Give him credit for more nous than that, sweetheart! He's hardly likely to boast about continuing something he's agreed not to do, now is he?'

'I guess not,' she had little option but to concede, pulling a dissatisfied face. Did Roman always have to shoot down her arguments with quite such efficient plausibility? 'But I'll still be asking Grandpa for his side of it, if for no other reason than to prove you wrong.' Green eyes connected challengingly with blue.

'You can live in hope,' he returned drily—his next

words making it plain he didn't. 'But while you're about it, I recommend you suggest he lays off, all the same. Otherwise, you never know but one of these days we may just be tempted, or riled enough, to retaliate.'

Not that Sheri altogether believed either of the McNamaras would—after all, both of them seemed as committed to the idea of a truce as her brother was, she had to admit—but at the same time she still didn't think it prudent to discount the warning too lightly either. When all was said and done, it would be a little one-sided to expect them to be the only ones to show restraint *if* her grandfather had gone back on his word.

A thought that was still uppermost in her mind when she returned home a short while later, and one that sent her hurrying to locate her grandparent as soon as she had changed into dry clothes. She found him deep in discussion with her brother in the lounge, and too anxious to have the matter settled promptly, she burst in on their conversation without ceremony.

'Grandpa, were you up to your old tricks on Castlewood yesterday?' she demanded more bluntly than she had intended, and had two astonished faces turning her way as a result.

Her grandfather was the first to recover, his surprise being submerged beneath an expression of assumed innocence. 'Now what tricks would they be, darling?' he teased.

Followed shortly by Chris's frowning, 'What on earth are you talking about, Sheri?'

With one last doubtful glance at her grandfather—at any other time she probably would have been amused by his artless pretence, but right at the moment it was more important she know the truth—she swung her gaze in her brother's direction.

'I—er—met Roman a while ago and he was telling

me that someone let all their stock out of their back paddock yesterday, and he apparently thinks it may have been . . .' she took a deep breath, 'it may have been Grandpa's doing,' half turning again in order to see the older man's reaction.

'Oh?' Colin's bristling brows peaked sardonically. 'Someone saw me, did they?'

Sheri could hardly withhold a gasp. Was he actually confessing, or—or just being sarcastic?

It seemed Chris wasn't soo sure either, because he promptly sought clarification from the man beside him by probing in a wary voice, 'Meaning?'

Their grandfather smiled complacently. 'Meaning, he wouldn't just be *thinking* it was me if someone had seen me, but since it's obviously just an assumption, then it's equally clear that he has no proof whatsoever.'

Which wasn't particularly enlightening at all! 'By that, then, are we to take it you're saying you did release their stock?' it was Sheri's turn to question cautiously, reluctantly, now.

He looked from one to the other of them with narrowing blue eyes. 'If that's what you want to believe, then go right ahead,' he recommended, but in a markedly less genial manner.

'Grandpa, please! Of course that's not what we want to believe!' She shook her head helplessly. 'But if you didn't do it, why can't you just come out and say so? Surely that isn't expecting too much. I mean, it must help to convince Roman if we could just tell him you'd denied it.'

'Because that's all you're interested in now . . . what Roman thinks?' he bit out roughly.

'No, of course not!' she cried, looking to her brother for support. 'All I'm interested in is being able to tell him I was right, and that you didn't have anything to do with his sheep getting loose.'

'And do you really think a mere denial will be sufficient to do that when my promise to end the feud obviously wasn't?' he retorted cynically.

Put like that she supposed it did sound rather illogical. 'I—well, it still wouldn't hurt, would it?' she proposed in weakening tones.

'Yes, it damn well would!' his answer came in no uncertain terms as he pushed himself to his feet. 'I gave my word and, as far as I'm concerned, that's all I have to say on the matter!' And with one last testy glare he went storming from the room.

'Oh, lord!' Sheri slumped down into her grandfather's recently vacated chair with a rueful grimace. 'I really made a mess of that, didn't I?'

Chris nodded explicitly.

'Well, I didn't hear you doing much to help,' she complained with a half laugh. Then, when he would have spoken, she waved a demurring hand and went on, 'Oh, don't worry, I know I didn't exactly give you much of an opportunity to say anything.' She looked towards the door her grandfather had just paced through, her expression wry. 'I'll wait for him to cool down a little and then I guess I'd better go and apologise. Whoever it was, it wasn't Grandpa who let those sheep out, was it?' Her eyes lifted remorsefully to her brother's.

He shook his head. 'No, I don't really think it was.' Stopping momentarily, his gaze became contemplative. 'Although I'd certainly be interested to learn why Roman apparently thinks it may have been.'

Sheri shrugged impassively. 'Mainly, I gather, because it was always a favourite practice of Grandpa's in the past, and because it appears there were no new tracks leading on to the property to indicate the gate had been opened for the purpose of gaining access,' she said flatly.

'Oh?' Chris's brows pulled together in a frown. 'That does make it interesting, doesn't it?'

'You're beginning to have doubts regarding Grandpa?'

'Well, I've got to admit it does start to make one wonder,' he mused, then followed it with a dismissive shake of his head. 'No, I still can't quite bring myself to believe it. There's no reason for him to want to begin the feud again.'

'Unless, of course, he's discovered what you and Roman are doing behind his back,' put in Sheri pointedly. Not surprisingly, it was a matter that was still at the forefront of her mind.

'Oh, that's where you came across Roman, is it?' her brother grinned comprehendingly. And, obviously distracted, 'So how's the work progressing?'

'Probably even faster now than it was before, considering what I had to say about it,' she grimaced tartly.

Chris eyed her askance, his mouth shaping ruefully. 'I don't think I like the sound of that.'

'I don't think Roman did either when I ordered him off the place,' she revealed on a rather sardonically defiant note.

'Oh, hell, you didn't!' Chris looked skywards in despair. 'He's doing that work as a favour to *me*, Sheri!'

'So he said,' she admitted in the same caustic fashion. 'But I still don't think you had any right to ask him to! Grandpa only said he was prepared to *talk* about the matter!' Her gaze was reproving.

'And so we have been,' he hastened to assure her. 'In fact, it was the groundwork we were discussing when you came in.'

'You mean, he knows that paddock's being cleared?'

His lips shaped into an irrepressible grin. 'Well,

let's just say he does now, even if he didn't a day or so ago when the work first started.'

The information at least allowed Sheri to utter a small sigh of relief. She hadn't liked the idea at all of her brother not telling their grandfather what was happening. 'Does he also know who's doing the clearing?' she enquired wryly.

'Uh-huh,' he confirmed laconically, giving her a teasing glance. 'And if I may say so, he seemed to accept the fact more equably than you apparently did.' Fortunately, from Sheri's standpoint, he didn't labour the point but continued almost immediately, 'And that's just another reason why I find it hard to believe he had anything to do with Roman's stock escaping.'

'Then if Grandpa didn't leave the gate open . . . who did?' Frowning, she looked to him for assurance. 'Or could it just have been a coincidental accident?'

Chris ran a hand through his hair thoughtfully. 'Since that's the only explanation that appears to be left, I guess that's what it must have been,' he shrugged.

CHAPTER EIGHT

As the week progressed, however, it soon became increasingly apparent that it had neither been a coincidence nor an accident, because as each day passed so other similar such offences were found to have been perpetrated, and even Sheri and Chris's belief in their grandfather's innocence began to waver somewhat in the face of his continuing refusal to even discuss the subject.

Not unnaturally, in consequence Roman's forbearance began to show definite signs of having run out, especially as each new attack proved more damaging than the last, but still Sheri hadn't been prepared for the news her grandfather had imparted one morning to the effect that whole panels of their own fencing had been cut in return.

Acrimonious accusations and counter-accusations had really flowed back and forth between the two families then, reminiscent of the feud at its worst, and although Roman flatly denied having done anything of the sort—he contended that Col had more than likely done it himself in an attempt to allay suspicion concerning his own efforts—Sheri found it impossible to believe him. After all, he'd told her himself that the McNamaras might retaliate if they became riled enough, she recalled, and he had certainly been that the day before on discovering paint had been thrown over one of their cotton modules waiting to be taken to the gin.

So when she awoke some time before dawn the following Friday, Sheri thought it was probably due to the tension of the preceding days causing her a restless night—until an experimental sniff told her that hadn't been the cause at all. Something was burning! And strongly too, judging by the amount of smoke and the red glow she now noticed was visible through her window, she realised in alarm as she threw off her bedcovers and hurried across the room to see.

Outside, the old machinery shed housing the ute and most of her grandfather's tools was firmly ablaze, no doubt fuelled by the oils and flammables stored there—although fortunately the property's petrol and diesel tanks were sited a safe distance away. Cursing the McNamaras for all she was worth—there were no doubts in her mind as to just how the fire had started—Sheri dragged her window shut to prevent any more of the acrid smoke getting into the room, then raced into the hall to alert the rest of her family.

Not that there was much any of them could do, as it was obvious the blaze already had too great a hold, but at least they could ensure it wasn't allowed a chance to spread, and by ceaselessly hosing everything within the vicinity of the building they were able to contain it until it eventually began to die down of its own accord.

In the meantime, Sheri's anger and disgust burned just as hotly as ever, and as soon as the main danger was past she knew there was only one way possible for her to get them out of her system. With this in mind she headed for the station wagon, luckily parked in the garage.

'Hey! Where on earth do you think you're going?' Chris called out in amazement a moment later to see her reversing into the yard.

'To give someone a piece of my mind!' she bit out between clenched teeth as she passed him, her foot already increasing its pressure on the accelerator.

With her irate thoughts to occupy her, the trip to Castlewood was swiftly accomplished, but after swinging wide the gate that had been the original source of all the present trouble, she hesitated before closing it again. Then, with a defiant toss of her head, she left it fully open and drove on. Why should she display any restraint after what they'd done that night? With luck, his damned sheep might find their way into the next Shire too this time!

And when she said *his* sheep, there was only one person she was meaning—Roman! The one she didn't doubt was behind the McNamaras' retaliatory actions, no matter what he claimed to the contrary! The one whose conduct was bringing tears of disappointment to her eyes right now because she had stupidly expected so much more of him, she suddenly realised in silent misery, brushing the back of an ash-stained hand across her damp lashes. And why? she forced herself to ask, mockingly. Because she'd become a victim of her own scheme to aggravate him, and had senselessly fallen in love with him instead! Not only that, but when she knew very well he already had a girl-friend waiting in the wings too! Oh, God, just how unthinking could she have been?

Ahead of her the outline of the sprawling Castlewood homestead was just visible as the sun's first rays threw a pink light over the horizon, but what did most to swamp Sheri's despair with a reviving anger were the lights she could see shining from the windows. Of course, after returning from carrying out their contemptible deed it probably wouldn't have been worth their while to go back to bed! she smouldered. No, they were doubtless having a drink to celebrate their victory! The very idea was so infuriating that in her hurry to confront them with it she almost tripped over the red-coated dog lying curled on the front steps, but after a hasty word to reassure the startled animal, she continued across the verandah to begin hammering on the closed door with clenched fists.

'What the blazes . . .!' The forceful expostulation came as Roman flung open the door, although Hayden wasn't far behind. Both of them already dressed, naturally! Sheri had time to notice rancorously. 'You! I'm surprised you've got the hide to show your face round here, you conniving little bitch!' he lashed at her scathingly, unexpectedly, before she had time to speak. 'Hell! Here we've been thinking your grandfather's refusal to deny our charges was just a cover-up for himself, when all the time it was little Miss Innocent he was shielding! Wasn't it, sweetheart?' He ground the words out with scorching sarcasm. 'I should have guessed after that episode with the keys just who was behind all the trouble! Well, tonight you outsmarted yourself. You didn't realise the ground round the tractor was damp, did you?' His mouth curved contemptuously. 'But that little mistake of yours allowed everything to fall into place, so now . . . if you don't mind,' catching hold of her upper arm in a vicelike grip he began propelling her towards the steps, 'I suggest you get off this property as fast as you can, before I forget you're a female!'

From having been staring at him incomprehendingly, Sheri now came back to struggling, indignant life. 'Oh, no, you don't, Roman McNamara!' she seethed as she battled to avoid being forced into her car. 'I don't know what the hell you're talking about with damp ground and things falling into place—or whatever—but you needn't think you're going to palm me off by confusing the real issue, or that you're going to get rid of me that easily either, you miserable bastard!' She beat wrathfully at his chest. 'To start a

fire in Grandpa's machinery shed like you did tonight,
you'd have to be lower than a snake!'

Grabbing both her wrists and holding her away
from him, Roman half laughed disdainfully. 'Fire!
What fire? *If* there was one,' he gibed on a scornful
note, 'it was probably started by Col in order to get a
new shed from the insurance company. He's wily
enough!'

'That's a lie!' she cried, her breath coming in
choking gasps as she continued to try to break free.
'We all know damned well who started that fire . . .
you did!' Her accusing eyes encompassed both of
them. 'And if the smell of smoke hadn't woken me
when it did, the whole place could have gone up!'
Abruptly, she felt the sting of salt beneath her eyelids
and unbidden tears spilled on to her glossy lashes as
she reserved her most bitter glance for the man
holding her. 'Or was that your intention?'

He shook his head wearily. 'Oh, for God's sake,
Sheri, why don't you just go home,' he urged, sighing,
and apparently gauging it safe to do so, dropped her
wrists and raked a hand through his hair. 'You've
caused enough trouble here tonight already. We don't
need any more. So if you'll just get in . . .' He opened
the car door.

'No!' She stood her ground, her chin angling
defiantly. 'And stop trying to make out I have
something to answer for! You're the . . .'

'*Make out* you've something to answer for! That's a
good one!' he cut her off harshly. 'You don't seem able
to understand, you left proof this time, sweetheart!'

'So you keep saying! But I still haven't heard yet . . .
proof of what?' she jeered, deciding to call his bluff.

This time when Roman shook his head, it was with
incredulity. 'You really do believe in brazening things
out, don't you, Sheri? But if that's the way you want

it . . .' He took hold of her arm again and began marching her towards a huge tractor stationed beside one of the outbuildings. 'There!' He stabbed a finger at a pile of some white substance on the ground next to the machine that she stared at bewilderedly. 'But of course that's only a small part of it, because the majority is already in here!' he rasped, slapping a hand resoundingly against the fuel tank. 'And do you know what sugar does to an engine like this, sweetheart? Well, naturally you do,' he answered his own question sarcastically, 'otherwise you wouldn't have put it in there, would you? But you wanted to see the proof of your involvement, I believe,' he went on in the same satirical tone. 'Well, take a good look at those,' pointing out some well defined footprints in the soil a little further along, 'and then maybe you'll admit what we've *known* ever since we first saw them!'

With the sun reaching higher by the minute, it was possible for Sheri to see the marks quite clearly, and it was obvious they had been made by a woman's shoe. The shape was most distinctive with its small tapering sole and rounded puncturing heel, and it was exactly because of those features that she turned defensively to Roman.

'All right, so the prints were made by a woman's shoe, I'll grant you that, but I certainly wasn't wearing them at the time!' she disclaimed fiercely. 'These are what I always wear around the property,' gesturing to her grandmother's stock boots showing below her jeans, 'but even if I didn't, I can assure you I wouldn't even contemplate carrying out something of this nature in the style of shoe that obviously is! Besides, you can see for yourself, those footmarks are much smaller than mine. In fact, I don't think I even *know* anyone with quite that small a foot.'

For a split second still partly suspicious blue eyes

clashed with defensive green, and then all of a sudden both their expressions began registering realisation, as if they had simultaneously arrived at the same conclusion, and with one hand forming a fist Roman punched it roughly into his other.

'Oh, yes, you do,' he claimed in a heavy voice. 'We both do. Don't we?' His brows rose meaningfully.

'N-Nerissa?' she hazarded faintly, just in case their thoughts weren't quite so aligned as she believed.

'Nerissa!' he repeated in a decisive tone and, expelling a long-drawn-out breath, touched the tips of his fingers fleetingly to her pale cheek. 'Well, well—now everything really does begin to fall into place, doesn't it?' His mouth took on a rueful slant.

'I guess so,' Sheri nodded, subdued by the thought of the damage the other girl had been prepared to cause in an effort to achieve her own ends.

'Mmm, she certainly played all of us off against each other . . . and very successfully too, I'm sorry to say,' he sighed wryly. 'At least, until she inadvertently left these footprints.'

'Which you promptly suspected were mine,' Sheri couldn't help but remind him in reproachful accents.

'I'm sorry.' Half smiling crookedly, he dropped an arm about her shoulders and began guiding her back to the house. And because she was so relieved to have had her faith in him restored, she made no move to dislodge it. 'But as I said, it all seemed to add up when we found those. It just never occurred to us—or any of you either, apparently—that it might have been an outsider. Unfortunately, we've had trouble between our two families for so long that it was a simple enough matter to have everyone automatically assuming it was the same ones taking part again.'

A contrite smile edged its way across her lips in response. 'I'm sorry too for accusing you of starting our fire.' She dipped her head selfconsciously as they rejoined his brother. 'When I saw the lights on I thought you couldn't have been back long and were still celebrating your success.'

'Bemoaning the work that's now going to have to be done on the tractor, more like,' grimaced Hayden eloquently.

'Well, it wasn't Sheri's doing,' Roman told him.

'No sweat, I already figured that,' was the dry return, accompanied by a significant glance for the placement of his older brother's arm. 'But if she didn't . . . who in blazes did?'

It didn't take long to explain, and after his initial astonishment, Hayden too was soon nodding his rueful understanding of the clever use of each family's one-time distrust of the other.

'And she really set fire to Col's shed tonight as part of the scheme, did she?' Hayden shook his head incredulously. 'S'truth! That's one dangerous female to cross!' with another expressive look at his brother.

'Yeah, well,' Roman's lips twisted ironically, 'since she did, maybe it wouldn't be a bad idea if you took yourself over there to see if you can lend a hand with the clearing up.'

Hayden accepted the suggestion with a casual nod. 'You want me to break the news, as it were, while I'm there too?'

'Perhaps I should be the one to do that, and preferably before you arrive,' put in Sheri anxiously. 'Right at present I'm sure Grandpa isn't feeling particularly kindly towards any McNamara,' with a speaking half smile, 'and his first instinct on seeing you could be to get his shotgun!'

'He'll manage. Chris will listen to reason even if Col doesn't,' Roman dismissed her concern with an easy negligence.

'Yeah, don't worry, Red, you can leave it to me,' Hayden added reassuringly as he tweaked a lock of her hair in the same manner as he had always done when they were children. A gesture that had her retaliating with only a mock direful gaze on this occasion, and him replying with the same impenitent grin of old.

'Well, as I have to go back anyway, I'll just follow him, then,' she said to Roman when the younger man had returned inside for his hat.

'Uh-uh! Not just yet.' He shook his head in veto. 'We still have things to discuss.'

'Do we?' She glanced up at him, perplexed.

'We do,' he smiled uninformatively, raising a casually acknowledging hand in response to Hayden's, 'I'll see you later,' as he re-emerged from the house and departed in their white ute.

Sheri watched the vehicle disappear with a sudden feeling of disquiet. For some unknown reason, she felt more nervous alone with Roman now than she had when she'd been preparing to charge him with arson!

'Will it take long?' she asked in a murmur that, to her dismay, sounded decidedly shaky.

'Why? Are you in a hurry to get back?'

She suspected he was mocking her, and was aware of a desperate need to defend herself. 'I'm expecting a phone call, actually . . . from Todd,' she lied with as much nonchalance as possible.

'At this hour?' he laughed in patent disbelief.

A rush of staining colour surged into her cheeks. How could she have forgotten just how early it still was? 'So?' she attempted to bluster her way out.

'So we may as well go inside to wait for it,' he caught her unawares by drawling as he urged her towards the steps. 'Once the exchange finds out where you are, they can put the call through here just as easily.'

'Yes, I suppose so,' she shrugged, allowing him to show her into a tastefully decorated sitting room without any further demur. Just knowing his housekeeper would be around somewhere made her feel distinctly easier.

'Have a seat,' he gestured to a large, comfortable-looking, wine-coloured velvet sofa, 'while I make some coffee. Or would you prefer tea?' His brows peaked enquiringly.

She shook her head slightly. 'No, coffee will do fine, thanks.'

'Or if you'd like to clean up, the bathroom's on the left at the end of the hall,' he grinned unexpectedly, and leant over the sofa to flick a teasing finger at her. 'You've got an ash smudge right across your nose.'

'Oh!' Sheri flushed pinkly, and when he continued on to the kitchen, made a beeline for the bathroom where she discovered, to her further embarrassment, that her nose wasn't her only feature to have been so blackened. Her forehead, her cheeks, and her chin were similarly marked as well. In fact, she looked an absolute wreck! she grimaced, before beginning to soap all traces of the disfiguring ash vigorously away.

Back in the sitting room once more, and feeling considerably more composed, she looked up questioningly on Roman's arrival with the coffee tray which he proceeded to place on a table beside the sofa. 'Isn't Dorrie awake yet?' she half smiled, half frowned. Thus far she'd neither heard nor seen a sign of his housekeeper.

Bending, Roman passed her the mug he had just filled, and shook his dark head lightly. 'She's not even here, as a matter of fact. She stayed the night in town with her sister's family after going to some get-together that wasn't expected to finish before midnight, and won't be back until later this morning.

That's why we were up earlier than usual when you arrived . . . to cook breakfast,' he smiled wryly.

'Oh, I see,' she acknowledged in a weak voice, helping herself to cream and sugar. So there was only the two of them there! Somehow she found the idea a little discomfiting. Then taking a steadying sip of her drink she squared her shoulders determinedly. Her anxieties were probably all groundless, anyway! 'Well, what was it you wanted to discuss with me?'

Roman stretched out in a commodious, matching armchair a few feet away, cradling his mug between tanned hands, and viewing her leisurely with his incredibly blue eyes. 'I think it's about time this pretence of ours came to an end,' he proposed slowly.

Sheri dipped her head quickly, pressing her lips together in an effort to hide their sudden trembling. Doubtless he was even more impatient to resume his relationship with Nerissa now, she supposed desolately. She hadn't missed the fact that his reaction to discovering his girl-friend had been the troublemaker had been nowhere near as explosive as when he had believed herself to be at fault! 'You're of the opinion it's served its purpose, then?' she parried in thickening accents.

'Uh-huh,' he drawled. 'Particularly in view of this morning's happenings and revelations. Don't you?'

'I—I . . . if that's what you want,' she whispered, feeling more disconsolate at the thought than she would ever have believed possible.

'Still letting someone else make your decisions for you, huh?' he gibed lazily.

'No!' She gazed at him with hurt eyes. How could he continue to say that when she had been refusing her mother's demands to return home all week? 'I was merely—merely going along with your suggestion, that's all.'

'The same as you'll eventually go back to Sydney and obligingly allow Heather to continue running your life for you exactly as before?' His tone roughened noticeably.

'You can't be s-sure of that,' she defended on a tremulous note.

'Can't I?' His mouth assumed a disparaging curve. 'Then what will you do?'

'Well, whatever I decide, it won't be of any concern to you, will it?' she cried distractedly. He'd just made that abundantly clear! She fought to regain at least a vestige of calm. 'Not that it's ever been any business of yours, in any event. And now, if you've quite finished,' the faintest touch of sarcasm entered her voice, 'I think I'd better be going.' Replacing her still almost full mug on the table, she rose swiftly to her feet.

Roman just as rapidly consigned his own mug to a smaller table nearer his chair, his fingers closing about her wrist when she would have swept past him, and effectively bringing her to a halt. 'Oh, but I haven't finished yet,' he said in a return to his previously drawling tone. 'As it happens, I've only just started.'

'So what else did you want to say?' Wary green eyes held provoking blue.

'Nothing much,' he shrugged idly, and then followed it with a totally unanticipated tug on her arm that had her tumbling helplessly down on top of him. 'They say actions speak louder than words, don't they?' he murmured as his lips, firm and compelling, came down on hers before she had an opportunity to recover.

With her head imprisoned against his shoulder and one arm pinned against his chest, Sheri could only struggle feebly to avoid his persuasive touch. Her efforts to retain control of her senses were no less a losing battle either as they reeled beneath the onslaught of feeling he aroused within her, and finally she stopped trying. It just wasn't possible to fight both him and herself—not when she loved him as much as she did—and neither did it even seem to matter that he would probably be back in Nerissa's arms tomorrow, because her whole being had suddenly become attuned solely to here and now!

She wanted to experience again the thrill of his exploring hands, the warm caress of his mouth as it trailed across her heated and responsive skin, and to be able to touch him in return. With shaking fingers she undid the top buttons of his shirt and tentatively slid her hand inside to savour the feel of his convulsively tautening flesh, the soft curling hairs of his chest, and to slowly explore the powerfully muscled width of his shoulders.

Shuddering, Roman raised his head slowly, his eyes heavy with a smouldering desire that was matched in hers as they locked, and he unhurriedly unfastened her shirt to expose her bare, swelling breasts to his gaze. It was only then that Sheri remembered she hadn't bothered with a bra in her urgency to dress that morning, but although her throat constricted involuntarily, still she made no move to cover herself, and when he caressed her breasts to an aching need and lowered his head to draw a rosy, jutting nipple into his warm mouth, she knew an exquisite torment that was entirely new to her and which had her trembling compulsively.

Roman caught her to him even more closely and pressed his lips to the rapidly beating hollow of her throat. 'Dear God, Sheri!' he ejaculated hoarsely. 'What are you trying to do to me? You can't possibly mean to go back to Sydney after this!'

Sheri closed her eyes in despair. So what did he

expect her to do? Share him with Nerissa? 'I'm s-sorry, but I don't believe in three-way relationships,' she just managed to get out.

His head lifted swiftly, his eyes narrowing. 'You mean, with this Todd of yours?' he demanded tightly.

'No! I mean with that Nerissa of *yours*, of course!' she sobbed, and averted her head as tears began flowing uncontrollably down her cheeks.

'Oh, hell, *love*!' he groaned achingly, turning her face back to his with gentle but inexorable fingers. 'Can't you tell when a man's in love with you ... and only you? Nerissa means nothing to me. Good lord, how could you possibly even begin to think otherwise after the trouble she's caused? Besides,' his lips slanted wryly, 'I broke off with her—permanently—when you agreed to go to the Ball with me. I guess I must have known even then that no matter what happened, I wouldn't be wanting to escort her anywhere again.'

For a time Sheri could only gaze up at him wonderingly, hardly daring to believe the avowal she had so longed to hear. There was so much she wanted to say that it was difficult to decide where to begin, but first, she realised, she had to get Nerissa out of the way once and for all. 'That isn't what you told me, though,' she part frowned, part accused bewilderedly.

'So I strained the truth a little,' he confessed with a slow, captivating grin. 'I wouldn't have wanted a certain saucy redhead believing it was going to be that easy to commandeer all my time, now would I?'

'Oh!' she smiled mistily, ruefully. 'And is that also why you sought her out at the Ball?'

'Uh-uh, I didn't seek her out, she called me over,' he corrected her assumption drily. 'And I could hardly refuse to speak to her.'

'You didn't have to look quite so pleased about it, though, did you?'

'If I did, I must be a better actor than I thought, then, because I certainly wasn't feeling particularly pleased about it at the time,' he half laughed.

A disclosure that cheered his listener considerably—until another point came to mind that had her eyes clouding doubtfully again. 'Nor did you look terribly disturbed on discovering Nerissa was the one behind all our present troubles,' she recalled. 'Not like what you had to say when you thought I was at fault.'

Roman's arms tightened about her possessively. 'Because it hurt like hell to think you might have been responsible,' he revealed in a deepening voice. 'When I realised you weren't, I was just so damned relieved I didn't really care much about anything else.'

With the last of her worries disposed of, the curve of Sheri's mouth widened delightfully. 'I thought you might have been flattered by the lengths she was prepared to go to in the hope of splitting us up,' she owned with a ruefully apologetic look.

'Flattered by them?' His disbelieving return glance spoke volumes. 'I'd like to flatten her for them! She came all too close to achieving her aim for my liking!'

For Sheri's too, and she nestled closer. 'But what will happen with regard to all the damage she's done?' she questioned thoughtfully.

'Unfortunately, nothing, I guess,' he sighed. 'Knowing something, and being able to prove it are two completely different things, I'm afraid, and in this instance I suspect it would be nigh on impossible.'

'Then what's to stop her continuing?' The thought had her biting at her lip apprehensively.

'Our marriage!' his reply came promptly, tenderly. 'I doubt even Nerissa could fail to get the message then!' Pausing, his eyes filled with an evocative warmth. 'And what a perfect reason for not waiting a moment longer than we absolutely have to!'

An answering glow appeared in the depths of Sheri's emerald eyes and she wound her arms adoringly about his neck. 'Oh, Roman, I love you, I love you!' she breathed fervently. 'I don't think I could live without you now!'

'Don't worry, princess, there's no way I'm likely to let that happen,' he reassured her in throaty tones. 'I love you, I want you, I need you,' he interspersed each declaration with a kiss to her eyes, her nose, her lips, 'and not only that, but even if Nerissa hadn't made it prudent, I also intend to marry you as soon as humanly possible in order to keep you by my side for the rest of my life! So don't say you haven't been warned!' His gleaming white teeth showed in an utterly fascinating smile.

No nicer or more desired warning could Sheri have ever received, as her loving reaction demonstrated, and it was some time before any extraneous thoughts intruded again. When they did, she still remained close within the circle of his protective arms.

'Won't Mother have something to say when she hears the news?' she mused lightly. Not even the thought of her parent's displeasure had the power to worry her now.

'And Todd,' added Roman in an indolently provoking drawl. 'It doesn't look as if he's going to ring you, after all, does it?'

Sheri buried her head against his shoulder selfconsciously. 'I only said that because I was scared you might guess how I felt about you otherwise,' she admitted in muffled tones.

'That's what I suspected . . . or at least, hoped!'

Looking upwards again, a slight frown began marking her forehead. 'But if that was how you—how you felt,' she faltered shyly, 'why did you suggest we stopped seeing each other, then?'

'Uh-uh.' He shook his head slowly. 'I suggested it was time our *pretence* came to an end. You may have assumed the other, but as you've no doubt guessed, that wasn't my intent at all. Why else do you think I accused you once again of allowing someone else to make your decisions for you, and tried to force you into agreeing not to return to Sydney?'

'I thought because . . .' Halting, Sheri dismissed the painful remembrance with a careless shrug. 'Oh, who cares what I thought! It's what I now *know* that's important,' she smiled radiantly as she followed the contours of his shapely mouth with the tip of her finger.

Catching hold of her hand, Roman pressed a lingering kiss to her palm. 'And don't you ever forget it!' he murmured roughly.

'I won't,' she promised, and leant back against him contentedly again. Suddenly her eyes began to sparkle with amusement. 'Isn't Chris going to be surprised, though, when he discovers I'll also be living in Goonagulla from now on?'

'Like hell!' His retort was drily expressive. 'Your dear brother has been having a good laugh at my expense for some time now.'

'You mean, he guessed how you felt?' she chuckled.

'He would have to have been blind not to,' he drawled mockingly.

'Oh?' Her arched brows rose interestedly.

A wry smile caught at the edges of his lips. 'You were right, you know, that first day when you accused me of wanting something from Chris in return for my having helped him.' His smile broadened disarmingly. 'I asked for his help in obtaining something I wanted . . . his sister.'

The completely unexpected revelation had Sheri sitting up rapidly and her eyes rounding in astonishment. 'But—but you'd only just met me again at the airport!' she stammered incredulously.

'And immediately recognised the girl I wanted to marry!'

It was unbelievable! 'So all this time the pair of you have been scheming together, have you?' She didn't know whether to feel pleased or outraged.

'Something like that,' Roman confessed readily.

'Oh!' she gasped in mock indignation. 'And you had the nerve to call *me* devious!'

'Well, so you were,' he charged with a rueful laugh. 'You had me going round in circles trying to figure out just what you were up to.'

'Good! I'm glad,' she grinned unsympathetically. 'It appears you deserved it even more than I thought— and when I get my hands on Chris . . .'

'You'll be very nice to my future brother-in-law,' he directed in a teasing, pseudo-menacing fashion.

'Well, since it hasn't turned out too un-satisfactorily . . .' She struck a considering pose.

'Mmm, if Nerissa only realised it, she's probably done us a favour by bringing matters to a head so swiftly,' he smiled with obvious pleasure. 'I very much doubt she imagined this would be the result when she decided to leave our gate open that day.'

The reminder had Sheri suddenly clapping a hand to her mouth in horror. 'Oh, my God, the gate!' she exclaimed, and in response to Roman's frowning look of incomprehension, disclosed abjectly, 'I—er—left it open when I came through because I was so mad at what I thought you'd done.' She shrank away from him as if expecting an explosion.

'Oh, no, not again!' His eyes closed in wry despair. 'Or maybe it won't be too bad,' he went on to speculate in a more hopeful vein. 'Hayden would have shut it when he went through.'

Sheri cleared her throat with a gulp and smiled apologetically. 'Most of the sheep were around the gate at the time, and—er—already moving on to the road when I left.'

'You little fiend! I ought to beat you!' he threatened with feigned ferociousness.

'I know,' she chuckled impishly, winding slender arms around him again and stretching up to place a conciliatory kiss to the corner of his sensuous mouth. 'But I'll help you muster them all again . . . I promise.'

For a while Roman seemed more interested in reciprocating the pressure of her clinging lips, but obviously feeling some reply needed to be made, he growled righteously, 'My oath, you will!' Then, returning his attention to what evidently attracted him most, his voice softened to a husky murmur as his mouth descended once more, 'But all things in order of importance, hmm?'

4 FREE
Harlequin Romances